Tales of the Golden Dragon

AIRSHIP 27 PRODUCTIONS

Tales of the Golden Dragon
© 2017 Barbara Doran

Published by Airship 27 Productions
www.airship27.com
www.airship27hangar.com

Interior illustrations © 2017 Gary Kato
Cover illustration © 2017 Rob Davis

Editor: Ron Fortier
Associate Editor: Gordon Dymowski
Marketing and Promotions Manager: Michael Vance
Production and design by Rob Davis.

ISBN-13: 978-1-946183-31-6
ISBN-10: 1-946183-31-8

Printed in the United States of America

10 9 8 7 6 5 4 3 2 1

Tales of the Golden Dragon

By Barbara Doran

Tales of the Golden Dragon

By Barbara Doran

Chapter One
Visitors are Cautioned to Avoid Strikersport Chinatown's Alleyways

"We're stuck."

"Yes, sir. I know. The customers are expecting a tour of the whole city, not just Chinatown."

"I know, tomorrow is the Hungry Ghost Festival and the only hotel in Chinatown is full up."

"And the bus is sitting right in the way of the parade."

"And, yes, Mr. Andersen is a Very Important Client."

"Whose Complete Satisfaction is Very Important to the Resort."

"And Mr. Striker and Mr. Jarvis will be Very Unhappy if Something Goes Wrong."

"I'll do my best, sir. I'm just not sure I can get a mechanic up here. Maybe if you—"

"No, I do understand. Keeping the tour on track is my job, not yours."

"I'll do my best, sir."

"I understand, sir."

Stephanie set the phone down as gently as she could, trying to keep from simultaneously crying and screaming. This job. This damned job. It'd seemed such a good idea, getting away from her overbearing family back in Detroit by running off to California at seventeen. Now, three years later, she wished she'd stayed home.

She'd tried to find work in Los Angeles, hoping for a chance in the movies. But there just weren't any roles for a half-black girl with a flat midwestern accent. Her looks weren't good enough and she wasn't willing to search for work in— traditional— ways.

Drifting north in search of decent employment, she'd landed in Strikersport, working as an assistant to Jewel Island Resort's public relations office. The resort was co-owned by John Striker and William Jarvis, scions of two of the town's richest families. Her direct boss was Perry Rose, a retired Colonel of the British Army. He was also the laziest man she'd ever met; more interested in his stamp collection than his work.

Mr. Rose's sloth meant Stephanie—officially his secretary—handled anything requiring effort. This job, taking a small group of out-of-town businessmen on a tour of Strikersport, was par for the course with him.

"Miss Frazier is angry?"

Stephanie looked at the speaker, a short Chinese man of indeterminate age and indefatigable good cheer, and couldn't help returning his smile. "No, Mr. Meow. I'm frustrated. I need to get the bus fixed and out of here."

"Mao."

Stephanie blinked, realizing the man was correcting the name she'd called him. "Isn't that what I said?"

"No, Miss Frazier. You said Me-ow. Mao means cat, so is funny, but still not my name."

Mao's correction was made without rancor or annoyance, but Stephanie took his point. She tried again, "Mao."

"Better. Close enough. Thank you." The chief cook and bottle-washer of Uncle Ip's Finestkind Chinese Restaurant bowed ever so slightly, adding, "May I make suggestion. Try next door." He waved his hand off to the side. "Can find help there."

Next door was the Jeen Loon, an import shop featuring the sort of bric-a-brac tourists loved. Carved lions, dragons, Buddha statues, jewelry, and delicate clockworks that rarely made it home in one piece. Stephanie had never been inside. Her apartment was too small and her bank account too meager to waste space or money on fripperies. "No offense, Mr. Mao, but I think a mechanic's shop would be a better choice."

"Finestkind mechanics at McLeod Motors," the cook said, as if that explained everything.

"I agree, and I'll probably call them first, but—"

Another broad smile. "Jeen Loon Chief Shopkeeper is Chou Chang. Also called Joseph McLeod. His father is owner of McLeod Motors. Chou prefers small things, but knows engines. If he cannot fix, his brother Robby can."

Now that was a different story altogether. Stephanie glanced into the dining room, where a small group of tourists in elegant clothes were eating. Three were missing, likely gone to the washroom, but the others were still gorging on the first course. She had time, she hoped. "Can you tell Mr. Andersen I've gone to do something about the bus? I'll be back as soon as I can."

Mao inclined his head. "Take this. *Cha siu bao*. You have not eaten yet."

He handed her a warm paper bag, then another. "That for Chou. Shrimp lo mein. His favorite."

Accepting both bags gratefully, Stephanie thanked the cook and headed out the door.

Jeen Loon Imports was a maze of delicate statues of wood, ivory, stone and gold, both fake and real. There was a faint, almost floral, scent in the air that reminded Stephanie of the temples and shops back in San Francisco's Chinatown. The sound of chimes tinkled softly as she entered, followed by an oddly metallic shriek. It took Stephanie a moment to realize it came from a radio sitting on a nearby counter, a metal dragon statue wrapped around it as if it were listening to the show. 'Sword of the Weaver Maiden' she thought it was.

At the center of the room, directly beneath an elaborate lantern of embroidered silk, was a case like those found in museums. A sign reading "Eight Immortals of Khaitan, ABSOLUTELY, POSITIVELY, NOT FOR SALE" was plastered on the sides. The last sentence was bright red and black and written in huge letters, suggesting the proprietor had had to say 'no' far too many times.

Inside the case, arranged at even intervals around a half-black, half-white circle, were eight statues carved from translucent black and white stone and decorated with gold and silver. They were amazing pieces of work, delicate figures of humans and beasts like monkeys, dragons and tigers.

"Welcome to the Jeen Loon," a young woman said and Stephanie turned to see a counter beside the door with a bored young Chinese girl doing what was obviously her homework. Whatever it was, it looked complicated, a series of geometrical figures and numbers, along with carefully written Chinese characters. The girl looked at Stephanie incuriously, adding, "Is there anything you're looking for specifically, or are you just browsing like the others of your group?"

Surprised, because she'd entered alone, Stephanie said, "Group?"

"Yes. Group. The ones you were with. I saw them go into Uncle Ip's with you earlier and there are three here now. Two women and a man with very red hair and little to say?"

Stephanie supposed she shouldn't be surprised. Mrs. Andersen and her companion, Minerva had picked at their food earlier and made noises about wanting to shop all morning. They must have gotten bored and come over to wait for the others. As for the third, he was most likely Mr. Rogers, Andersen's skinny, eminently forgettable secretary and dogsbody, dragged along to carry the shopping. So far Stephanie hadn't heard a peep out of him.

"They're with my group, yes, but I came to speak with Mr.— Chang was it?" She tried to remember the pronunciation and was relieved when the girl didn't flinch.

"You'll have to wait for the others to be done," the girl said and Stephanie thought there was a touch of exasperation in her voice. "They got to him first." She waved her hand towards the back.

Based on her morning with the group, Stephanie guessed the women were causing trouble. A perfect topper to a frustrating morning spent dragging her charges through breakfast at the resort, onto the ferry and a tour of the Strikersport Sentinel. She just hoped the paper's owner, Miss Trendle, hadn't taken offense at Andersen's scoffing disbelief at the idea of a female editor.

Heading towards the back of the shop, Stephanie heard the discussion before she reached it. Inevitably, it was Mrs. Andersen putting up the fuss. "I just don't understand how you can sell a statue and not know what it is."

"This ignorant clerk has told you, statue is *shi shi*, a stone lion. Specifically, it is *shi shi* cub. Most unusual to find without parents." From his tone, something obviously puzzled the shopkeeper, though he didn't say what.

"Then why did you tell Minerva it's a *fu* dog?"

"Beg pardon, but this foolish and confused one did not—"

"Because it's obviously a *shi shi*."

"Yes, most assuredly. It is *shi shi*. But it is not—"

"Well all I can say is you are being horribly deceptive, trying to make my poor friend think she was buying a *fu* dog."

Coming around the corner of a shelf, Stephanie saw a tall, skinny, and surprisingly broad-shouldered young man standing behind the counter, staring down at the two women with the blankest of expressions. From what Mr. Mao had told her, Stephanie was sure this was Chou Chang, or Joseph McLeod. His dark brown hair was cropped short, sticking up from his scalp like a brush. His features were fine-boned, but not quite Chinese, making his mixed blood obvious. His outfit, patterned blue silk jacket and loose black pants, were the stereotypical Chinese shopkeeper's garb.

By comparison, the two women talking to the young man were short, with elegantly coiffed overly blond hair and the sort of makeup job that took years to master. Neither were young, but their features were smooth and apparently unlined. They looked almost the same, with similar dark blue dresses, dark blue satin hats with poufy lavender flowers and dark blue stiletto heels.

Mrs. Andersen tapped the statue she held with a blue-tinted talon and Stephanie peered at it curiously. It was a ceramic lion cub, curled up in a way that put Stephanie in mind of a frightened puppy. "Well? What do you propose to do about this?"

"Am most humbly sorry to offend. Statue is *shi shi*. One we do not sell—"

"Nonsense. Everything has a price. What do you want for it?"

Chou blinked. "But statue is not ours. We do not sell such cheap merchandise—"

"I said, how much, young man and I expect an answer."

With a look suggesting he no longer cared, Chou told her, "Very well. Cost is twenty American dollar. You buy or not?" From the young man's tone, he'd obviously had quite enough of the fuss. Nor could Stephanie blame him. She'd have snapped by now, given he was being blamed for something he hadn't done.

Before Mrs. Andersen could open her mouth to add to the offense, Stephanie stepped in. "There you are, Mrs. Andersen. I was wondering if you were all right. You hardly touched your food."

"I came to shop with Minerva and this young man—"

Cutting the lady off as smoothly as she could, Stephanie said, "Yes, I quite understand. But English is obviously not his native tongue. I've no doubt you've confused the poor man into misunderstanding what you wanted."

A flash of annoyance crossed Mrs. Andersen's attractive features and Stephanie wasn't sure if the woman would turn on her instead. Then, perfectly painted lips tight, she set the statue under discussion on the counter slightly harder than necessary. Stephanie thought she saw a crack form in the delicate surface.

Chou Chang took the statue before Stephanie could open her mouth, saying, "Will be twenty dollar. You pay cash, please. No check." His fingers stroked it gently, as if he were soothing a frightened pet.

"For a damaged *shi shi* statue you tried to pass off as a *fu* dog?"

"Most humbly sorry to disagree. Did not call statue *fu* dog. Also, statue not damaged, ma'am." Chou turned it in his hands, showing the woman the piece without letting her touch it.

"It most certainly—" Mrs. Andersen's voice trailed off as she realized the statue was in perfect condition. Stephanie blinked, because she would have sworn there was a crack as well. "There was— I was sure—"

With a serene smile, Chou said, "Twenty dollar, no holler, ma'am."

Slowly, obviously furious at being thwarted, Mrs. Andersen drew a crisp twenty from her wallet and, once Chou had placed the statue in an elegant box, took her prize and handed it to Mr. Rogers. He'd been overlooked again thanks to the stronger personality of his employer's wife. Red hair aside, he was as non-descript as a store mannequin, his only distinction being a delicate topaz lapel pin carved to resemble a rearing horse.

"You know what to do with this, Rogers," Mrs. Andersen ordered. "Miss Frazier, I do hope we will be moving on soon. Please see to it. Come along, Minerva." She turned and left the shop without looking back, Minerva and Rogers following behind obediently.

As the women left, Chou muttered something in Chinese, an imprecation, Stephanie was sure. Then he turned and smiled at her, "I smell Mao's lo mein," he said in much better English than before. "And I have a feeling you wouldn't have come here with that, and his best *cha siu bao*, if he hadn't sent you. So, whatcha need?"

The sudden switch from extremely accented, even stereotypical Hollywood broken English, to the near perfect speech Stephanie associated with younger inhabitants of San Francisco's Chinatown was startling. Handing Chou the lo mein, she said. "Our tour bus broke down in the street outside the restaurant. I know it's in the way, but I can't ask my passengers to push it clear. Not to mention we're supposed to be visiting the winery and the casino later."

"The street's supposed to be cleared for the festival tonight anyway," Chou told her, peering over the shelves through the window. "Mao sent you here to fix it, huh?"

"If you can."

"No guarantees. Engines are more my brother Robby's thing." Chou gestured towards the back of the shop. "Let's eat and you can tell me what happened. If I can't fix it, I'll call big brother. He owes me one, anyway."

"As long as it's repaired before my group gets impatient, I don't care if the mechanic's a one-armed paperhanger or a monkey."

"The paperhanger's a better choice." Chou grinned as he led Stephanie into the back room. "You can never trust Monkey to stay on task."

Cha siu bao turned out to be soft, fluffy, steamed buns filled with a sweet, meaty, substance. Pork, according to Chou, combined with various sauces and vegetables. They were also Stephanie's new favorite food, she decided. She'd have to learn to pronounce it correctly, so she could order it again.

Chou took little time sucking down his lo mein noodles. It was a prodigious feat, one Stephanie could only compare to her older brother's ability to down several dozen hotdogs and half a gallon of milk in one sitting. "Where do you put all that?" she asked, cleaning her fingers. Aside from the shoulders, Chou looked long and bony. Moore, at least, turned all his food to obvious muscle.

"I perform at the theater at night," Chou told her. "Takes it out of you." He put his container in the trash and gestured for the door, taking off his outer coat to reveal a dark blue turtleneck. "We'd better get going. I doubt your friends will wait much longer."

They went out into the street, where a few dozen children had gathered around Stephanie's vehicle to stare at the thing. It'd been Mr. Rose's idea, a pink and white tour bus with the words, "Jewel Island Resort", emblazoned on its sides in intense black letters. Mr. Striker had winced when he'd first spotted it but by then the vehicle had already been paid for. Mr. Striker was a practical man who hated wasting time and money, so all he'd said was, "You needn't be too careful with it, really."

Chou sniggered at the sight. "I should see if I can get one like this." He shooed the children out of the way so he could get at the engine. When he opened the hood, however, he started choking, taking several steps back. "Oh, that's not good. That's not good at all." A cloud of black smoke followed him and he swatted the air covering his mouth.

Before Stephanie could ask the young man what the problem was, he set to work, ordering the children around him to help in rapid-fire Chinese. Within minutes the sound of clanging and swearing filled the air as Chou unbolted brackets and squeezed his way down towards whatever the problem was.

Realizing she was no use here, Stephanie told Chou, "I'll go check on my group. Send someone to get me if you need anything."

"Uh huh. Gotcha." Chou was already underneath the bus's chassis, so all she could see were long, gangly legs clad in loose black pants. It was obvious he was thoroughly involved in repairs. Obvious, too, that it would take a while. She might as well see if Mr. Andersen and the others would like to walk around.

When Stephanie entered the restaurant, however, Mr. Andersen immediately demanded, "What did you do with my wife?" He was a prim and proper Bostonian: just a bit past fifty, with carefully groomed brownish hair and mustache and surprisingly intense blue eyes. His old wealth didn't require him to be a snobbish, self-absorbed, git, but it didn't prevent it, either. From the first he'd treated Stephanie like a house-servant and his companions—being his employees—had readily followed suit.

Startled, because it'd been at least half an hour since Mrs. Andersen and her companions had left the Jeen Loon, Stephanie said, "I thought she was with you."

"You went over to that little trinket place next door to find her, didn't you? Her and her sister and that damnfool secretary of mine!"

"I'd gone to see about getting a mechanic for the bus, actually," Stephanie said, to explain why it'd taken her so long. "Mrs. Andersen and the others left just after I arrived. I thought she came back here."

"Nonsense. Do you see any sign of her in here?"

Managing not to say it was obvious Mrs. Andersen hadn't returned, Stephanie said placatingly, "I'm sorry, sir. I just meant—"

"You need to do something about finding her!" Andersen snapped, interrupting before Stephanie could finish her explanation. "I refuse to leave until she's back. Not to mention I need my secretary."

Stephanie sighed. "I understand. I'll call the police—"

"You will do nothing of the sort." At Stephanie's confused expression, the man added, "I won't have my personal business made public by bringing in those sorts of people. You just see about finding my wife. Ask around. She probably went looking for another place to spend my money on another broken toy. It is, after all, her favorite pastime."

Having no good reason to argue the point, Stephanie agreed. "I'll do my best, sir."

Once again, she went outside. Maybe Chou would have some idea of what to do.

Chou was entirely beneath the bus by the time Stephanie came back out, so all she could see were the soles of his feet. She was surprised to realize he was barefoot; somehow she'd failed to notice until now. Yet she didn't have time to ask why. Not when Mrs. Andersen had to be found.

"Chou? Are there any other gift shops in Chinatown?"

"What? You think mine isn't enough?" Chou's voice was muffled, both by virtue of the fact that he was halfway tangled in the bus's underworks and because he was banging on a pipe for some reason.

Stephanie sighed. "That's not it. Mrs. Andersen—the lady who bought the statue—and her companions, Miss Minerva and Mr. Rogers, have gone missing. They've probably gone shopping elsewhere, but—"

"Woman."

"What?"

"That was no lady, Miss Frazier. Either of them."

Smiling, because she couldn't exactly disagree, Stephanie said, "Either way, Mr. Andersen's—worried—and wants me to find them. I hate to interrupt your work, but—"

Crawling out from the works of the car, his cheek smudged with oil and his undershirt filthy with dust, Chou said, "You want me to interpret."

"Would you mind?"

"I can't think of anyone I want to find less than that—person—," Chou admitted. "But I've hit the end of my abilities with engines here." He turned to a little girl who was playing with one of his wrenches, swinging it like a club and narrowly avoiding hitting her watchful big brother. Taking the tool away, he spoke in Chinese.

The two nodded and ran off quickly, their short, strong legs carrying them down the road past the big stone pillars guarding Chinatown's entrance. When Stephanie looked at Chou, he grinned, "I sent them to get Robby. If anyone can fix that mess, he can. I'd have phoned, but they never hear it in the shop. Easier to send the kids."

Watching the children disappear down the hill below Chinatown, Stephanie hoped they'd be quick. The sooner they were done with this mess, the better. She turned back to Chou and was startled to realize the young man had cleaned himself up with amazing speed. The smudge on his cheek was gone and while there was still oil under his fingernails and he was probably filthy beneath his turtleneck, the high collar concealed the mess.

"There's a grocery up the way." Chou pointed. "They don't have much for tourists, but some of the townsfolk shop there. We should try it first."

Stephanie agreed, hoping he was right.

While there was no sign of their quarry, Stephanie's charges left a trail of confusion behind them wherever they went, making it easy to follow them. Or, rather, to follow the ladies. Mr. Rogers had either gone unnoticed or had wandered off somewhere. Given how non-descript he was, Stephanie suspected the former.

By contrast, no one could have ignored Mrs. Andersen or Minerva. One old man who'd dealt with the pair complained long and indignantly about Mrs. Andersen's attempt to buy his pet cricket, cage and all. The young grocery clerk was in tears over Minerva's complaint that she smiled too much. Further down the way, the bookstore owner was still scratching her head over the idea that a Chinese bookstore, in Chinatown, should sell only English works.

As far as Stephanie and Chou could tell, the priest of *Chiming* temple at the center of town had fared better. Bent over his prayers, his saffron hooded robe concealing his body completely, he was so focused on his duties he didn't notice anything else, including Chou and Stephanie. Seeing no point in disturbing him, Chou put a finger over his lips and gestured outside. "They can't have been here," he told Stephanie. "The Buddha himself couldn't have ignored those two."

Then there was the tailor shop, whose proprietor was puzzling over an order for a full dress kimono. The baker—whose mooncakes had been tasted and tossed to the ground as disgusting—was so furious he'd had to be forcibly restrained from taking his rolling pin and going after the pair. The capper had been in the town hall's courtyard, where Mrs. Andersen had tried to give the old man sunning himself there a few coins, assuming he was a beggar.

"Which, of course, you kept, didn't you, *Gong Gong*?" Chou accused.

The expression on Cheh Chang's face was impossibly innocent. "The possibility exists that I did, my impertinent grandson. As if you would not." His resemblance to Chou was such that Stephanie wasn't surprised they were related. They shared the same brush of hair and sharp-boned features, combined with a quirky smiles suggesting puckish humor.

Chou chuckled. "As you say, the possibility exists." He bowed to his grandfather, adding, "Do you know where they went? This lady is in charge of their group and wishes to find her missing goslings. There was also a man: a red-head named Mr. Rogers."

"The man was not with them when they visited." Chang shrugged dismissively. "As for the women, the one spoke of searching for more interesting things to do in— what was it she said— 'the authentic Chinatown'. I did suggest it was unwise, but for some reason they chose to ignore me. Perhaps they did not speak Chinese?"

Stephanie winced. She'd warned the group that while Chinatown's main street was safe enough, tourists shouldn't wander its alleys. For that matter, the rest of Chinatown really had nothing tourists would want to see. "I wish you'd stopped them," she said. "They're impossible, but Mrs. Andersen's husband is a big noise back in Boston and—"

"Miss Frazier, I have given orders to see to their safety and will amend them to include this Mr. Rogers," Chang said, surprising Stephanie by knowing her name. "I cannot guarantee every corner will be safe, of course, but there are few who would argue with me or my men."

"Only a few?" Chou asked archly.

"Almost none at all, impertinent youngling. Everybody loves Chang."

Stephanie turned to Chou. "I can't just leave them to their own devices, though. If you don't mind looking a while longer?"

"I don't mind, no." Chou bowed to his grandfather and made a proper farewell before leading Stephanie back out onto the street. "To tell the truth, I'd like to get those two out of Chinatown quickly. They're trouble we don't need, especially today. The Feast of Hungry Ghosts is not the time for ignorant outsiders to wander around aimlessly."

Chinatown's back streets weren't interesting to most tourists. They looked, for the most part, like any city's tenements. There were signs, here and there, all in Chinese. Little tiny shops whose windows were plastered with flyers and advertisements, all incomprehensible to Stephanie. They were also a tangled maze only a native like Chou could have navigated.

As before, Mrs. Andersen left a trail of disgruntled shopkeepers and residents behind her. That created another problem because each and every offended party insisted on explaining to Chou, in detail, just what the outsiders had done to offend. Which, for the most part, was the same thing each time. Arrogant certainty of one's welcome and supremacy seemed to be Mrs. Andersen and Minerva's hallmarks. Not to mention a deplorable inability to differentiate between *fu* dogs and *shi shi*.

"I'm sorry," Chou said as they rounded another corner, having detached him from an old woman who'd spoken so rapidly and incoherently Stephanie suspected even Chou had had difficulty understanding her. "They think of me as being Grandfather's stand-in. *Gong Gong* can be terribly lazy, sometimes."

By now the street they were on was deep inside Chinatown's southeastern quarter, the dingy grey stone showing no sign at all of shops. There'd been no sign of the two women, either, but this was the only way they could have come. Stephanie wondered what they were up to, so deep in a residential area. "There's nothing here for tourists, is there?" she asked Chou.

The young man looked worried. "Not as such, no. This isn't a part of town they should be at all. It gets rough."

As if to prove him right, a Chinese man, about Chou's age, crashed through a second story window in an alley. At the same time a small group came running up, shouting in Chinese, trying to help him stand. Somewhere above them, more men shouted and Stephanie was startled to hear English. "There he went! Out that window!"

What was more disturbing, though, was the sound of a woman's angry voice coming from that same apartment, its querulous tones all too recognizable. A moment later a dozen white men, oddly well dressed given their obvious occupation, rushed down the fire-escape after the youth and his friends.

As the fight broke out, Stephanie pointed at the window. "That sounded like Mrs. Andersen." Spotting the entrance to the apartment building, she rushed inside, despite Chou's attempt to stop her.

The young man caught up with Stephanie as she rushed up the stairs. "This isn't safe. Wait outside and I'll do what I can."

"No. Mrs. Andersen is my responsibility. I can't leave her." To tell the truth, Stephanie had no idea how to help the woman, but she'd lose her job if she didn't try. She didn't like Mr. Rose but she didn't want to crawl back to Detroit a failure, either.

Chou signed. "Then let me go first." His long legs had gotten him ahead of her anyway, so Stephanie didn't argue the point. Instead she followed grimly, unsure of what to do but determined not to leave her charges to be hurt or killed.

It was easy to tell where the thugs—and they were obviously thugs—had come from. Every door in the hallway was tightly shut but one and Mrs. Andersen's angry complaints were almost as good as a fire alarm. Chou stopped short of the doorway, keeping Stephanie from rushing in. "Wait," he whispered. "Let me make sure the coast is clear." Before she could object, he rolled into the room beyond.

Unsure what to do, Stephanie stayed where she was and wondered how to help if Chou was hurt.

It felt like forever, kneeling beside the door, listening to the sounds of fighting. Some came from the apartment, incoherent shouts and bangs that made Stephanie fear for Chou's life. The rest was outside, down in the alleyway.

A minute after Chou disappeared into the apartment, the door across the way cracked open and a tiny child, gender uncertain, age barely three, peeked out. Stephanie gestured at the little one, hoping they'd take a hint and get back and out of sight. Instead of obeying, the child held out a big wooden stick.

"Go back. It's not safe," Stephanie hissed, hoping the child would understand. But they held the stick out with a wide-eyed innocent look until Stephanie realized they wouldn't go away until she took the thing.

It wasn't just wood, she realized. Bands of yellow metal—brass, surely—around a lacquered reddish brown wood. Whatever it was, it was heavy, almost too heavy, for her to lift. She held it, unsure what to do.

The sound of someone running up the steps made Stephanie turn as a muscular man rounded the corner. From his appearance, he was one of outsiders. A white man, plain-faced and clean-shaven, he was as well-dressed as the others. At six foot tall with corresponding muscles, she knew he could knock her out with a flick of his little finger. Or, she noted with a sharp surge of fear, the iron chain swinging in his muscular fist.

There was nowhere to go. The hall ended just beyond the door where Mrs. Andersen's kidnappers were fighting. From the sound of things inside, she'd be sticking her borrowed staff into a hornet's nest if she tried to enter. Nor could she dodge into the room across the way, even though the door was still slightly open. The child inside might be hurt.

Staring at the man, Stephanie wondered if she could talk herself out of this. "I'm not—"

He rushed forward and Stephanie found herself taking several steps backward, so one foot was forward, the other behind. Without knowing what she was doing or why, she dropped into a slight crouch. To her terror, the man swung his fist, his weapon whistling as he moved.

Before Stephanie could scream or dodge she found herself thrusting the staff forward and sideways. The chain slammed into the staff, clanging like a huge bell, and wrapped itself around the end. Quickly, she twisted the weapon down and around, then thrust it forward, straight into her attacker's belly.

Stephanie barely stood five and a half feet tall and she was neither heavy, nor strong. She didn't need to be. As soon as the staff struck, it extended itself, growing from six feet long to an impossible sixteen. The force of the blow sent her attacker flying backwards and he crashed into the far end of the hallway. Immediately, an old woman stepped out of one doorway and slammed a wok onto the man's head, knocking him out before he could recover.

Stephanie stared, mouth agape, as the staff meekly returned to its former length. Then her bewilderment was interrupted by someone saying, "Get him!" "Stop that little—" "Where the hell did he go?" The voices came from the room Chou had entered. Realizing the young man might be in trouble, Stephanie stepped to the doorway.

Three men—her attacker's cohorts—were trying valiantly to subdue a fourth. They were armed with knives, trying to get a good cut in on their opponent and missing as the man dodged and twisted, swinging a slender staff with a brilliant purple flag attached to one end.

The last man was yet another stranger, though something about his appearance was familiar. Hadn't someone been telling her an outrageous story about a pair of masked avengers calling themselves the Claws of the Golden Dragon?

Whomever he was, he was dressed in a black, Chinese style, robe with flowing sleeves, his long black hair swinging in a queue, a strange blue mask painted on his face. The last looked like the sort of thing the Chinese actors at the Fragrant Mountain Theater wore, with odd blue and silver designs concealing his features.

Looking further into the room, Stephanie saw two women slumped on a ratty old couch. They were Mrs. Andersen and Minerva, both most fortunately unconscious. As for Chou, he was nowhere to be seen and Stephanie hoped he hadn't been hurt.

One of the men spotted her and changed targets. Except, yet again, Stephanie found herself reacting, dropping into that same crouch and swinging the staff in an arc that struck the man in the temple with the back end. Before he could recover, the staff swung again, slamming him on the other side and knocking him on his butt. The man in the blue mask kicked him in the back of the head, knocking him out.

The two remaining men stared from the masked man to Stephanie and back. Then one asked, "Are we getting paid enough to fight Dragon and this chick?"

"We most definitely are not."

"Let's scram then. Before Tiger shows up too and thoroughly minces our hash." The two men ran for the window and a minute later Stephanie

" . . . SLAMMED A WOK ONTO THE MAN'S HEAD . . . "

heard yells and squalls outside as the men dropped into the brawl in the alleyway.

The masked man went to the window and leaned out, shouting, "Tell Horne to stay out of Chinatown!" Then he turned to look at Stephanie. "Better give that back now. Before you owe the Great Sage more than you're willing to pay," he said in a quiet whisper.

"I don't understand any of this."

"If you're lucky, you will not have to." Somehow, the man folded his weapon and hid it in his capacious sleeve, adding, "Chou's in the bedroom, nursing a headache. Be nice to him. He was outnumbered, after all." He disappeared in a swirl of dark purple mist.

After checking to make sure the two women were alive, Stephanie went to find Chou just waking up. He'd been struck across the side of his face and it looked like he'd have a lovely black eye, but he seemed alright aside from that.

Something tugged at the back of Stephanie's skirt and she started, turning around fast, expecting to find another attacker. Except it was the little child, smiling at her with a broad and innocent grin, hand out towards the staff they'd loaned her.

"Oh— Yes. Sorry. Thank you." Stephanie didn't know what the thing was, nor how it'd done the things it'd done, but she was grateful for the help. She handed the staff back and forced herself not to gape as the child squeezed it down to a mere toothpick. Before she could stop the youngster, they reached up and stuck it behind her ear. It was so light she barely noticed it was there.

"You'll need it a while longer." The child grinned broadly, stepping back so Stephanie couldn't return the thing. "You'll know when."

Chou said, "You're loaning it freely. No price, Wukong."

"This time." The child let out a laugh that reminded Stephanie of a zoo and somersaulted backwards, disappearing in a flash.

Before Stephanie could open her mouth to say a word, a voice came from the outer room. "Well now, what's all this, then?" She didn't need to look to know it was the police.

"And that's all I really know, Officer Maloney." Stephanie watched the officer's partner checking Mrs. Andersen and her companion. The woman's yelling had gotten the two knocked unconscious and they were only now coming to. Meanwhile, Chou was sitting at a rickety old dining table, a bag of ice against his eye, looking very sorry for himself indeed.

Returning her attention to the heavy-set red-haired police officer, Stephanie continued, "I'm just glad you got here so quickly." She wasn't, actually, since she knew Mr. Andersen had expressly requested they keep the police out of the matter. He was the sort to take offense at her failure to comply even though there was good and sufficient reason.

"We were already here, lass. Some other little thing down at *Chiming Temple*," Officer Maloney grinned as Chou looked up at him with wide, startled, eyes. "There was a Tiger on the loose, among other things. And some idols stolen from the Jeen Loon." The last was said with a mildly embarrassed tone that made Stephanie wonder if there was more to the story.

"This one is most confused and grateful you came to help," Chou said, going back to his imitation of a Hollywood stereotype. "This one trusts there was not too much damage done, by either your honorable selves or that unprincipled character?"

The other officer, a well-tanned young man who looked like he might be of native blood, gave Maloney a malicious and significant smile. Voice oddly harsh for someone so young, he said, "I wouldn't say Tiger's too happy right now, but that had something to do with someone who, and I quote, 'doesn't know when to leave well enough alone.'" That elicited a glare from Maloney as Officer Kenneth stood up. "These two will be fine, though I think the one should stop drinking so much. It's not healthy."

"And you're the expert on healthy, are you, Gilly Kenneth?" Maloney waved his hand to stop his partner's answer. "Not another word from you. I'm in no mood for your backtalk right now."

About that moment, Mrs. Andersen roused completely, complaining furiously over her mistreatment and promising all sorts of retribution against the ones who'd grabbed her and her companion. Minerva added her voice to the litany, because the toughs who'd grabbed the two women had not only torn her pretty satin jacket but lost her good hat. The fact that they were safe and relatively uninjured after all that seemed to go entirely unnoticed.

With a sigh, Stephanie went back into work mode. "Now, now, I know this has been a terribly stressful time and you have my complete sympathy. We can stop at the nearest department store on the way to the winery if you'd like. Then you can get a whole new wardrobe, at the resort's expense, since you were under our care when this terrible thing happened."

Bending over backwards to make a customer happy wasn't something

Stephanie enjoyed, especially when it involved licking muddied boots and generally accepting blame for what wasn't her fault. It was, however, expected of her and she knew what would happen to her job if Mrs. Andersen wasn't satisfied.

Fortunately, though both women complained all the way back down to Uncle Ip's, the prospect of a new outfit and a trip to a winery for a garden party was enough to soothe their ruffled feathers. Relieved, Stephanie thought the rest of the day would be much quieter. After all, what sort of trouble could this lot find at a winetasting?

But why was it she felt like she was forgetting someone?

Chapter Two
Sentinel Journalists are Known for their Tenacity

Strikersport's Chinatown had always puzzled Simon Lee. Unlike the one in San Francisco, or his native New York, it was about as far from town as it could be and still belong to it. In fact, when it'd first been established, around the 1890s, it'd been over a mile from the city limits. It'd taken Strikersport sixty years to grow big enough to reach the enclave's western side.

In many ways, Chinatown was practically a stronghold behind a blank wall hiding its inhabitants from curious eyes. No cannon or weapons, of course, the white inhabitants of Strikersport would never have put up with such a thing. Yet Simon could never approach the place without being reminded of *Baimaguan* Fort, back near his grandmother's hometown. There was even a tower over the entranceway, featuring a pair of fierce looking looking stone guards.

Granted, the place wasn't nearly as big and impressive as *Baimaguan*, but it was still an unexpected thing to find in an American city, even one as odd as Strikersport. Abutting Strikers Peak, it was built on a flattened plateau overlooking Gold Dust River, its stone walls blank and forbidding, the only entrance the west-facing Dragon Gate. Lee had read that the Striker family had sold the land to the current Mayor's father for a few hundred dollars, back in the early 1890s. Not long after a landslide had shattered half the mountain and destroyed Striker's first mining camp. There were rumors some of the mine shafts were still there beneath Chinatown, a maze to rival the one in San Francisco.

Realizing he was procrastinating, mostly because he never felt comfortable with its inhabitants, Simon drove in, intending to find a parking place. Except his path was blocked by that godawful tour bus from the Jewel Island resort, the one painted to resemble a giant 'good and plenty'. Lee always felt sorry for Miss Frazier, who had to drive the monstrosity, but he couldn't help cursing her parking.

Parking as far to the side as the bus would let him, Simon got out in time to hear a stream of profanity combining English, Gaelic, Mandarin, Cantonese, and some dialect he didn't recognize at all. Recognizing Robby McLeod's voice, he peered under the bus to find the oldest son of McLeod Motors struggling with a bracket. "Are you all right?"

"No. No, I am not. That brat brother of mine ordered me to fix this thing and ran off to play." Robby pulled an object out from beneath the engine, adding, "After, of course, trying to fix it himself and making things worse! He's taken everything apart except the thing that's not working, for reasons known only to himself. Typical!"

Simon knew Robby better than Chou, mostly from their work at the radio station or from his taking Miss Trendle's limousine to the shop for maintenance. From what little he'd seen of Robby's flighty little brother, Chou was a quirky youth who enjoyed pulling Robby's chain, so the long-winded complaint wasn't surprising.

"I'd offer to help," Simon said, "But I have a job. You wouldn't happen to have noticed where the tour group this vehicle belongs to has gone?"

"Chou's chasing a few of them through the city, or so they tell me. I think the rest of the lot are over in Uncle Ip's." Robby slid out from under the car. He was a tall, broad-shouldered man just barely nineteen. Light skinned and dark-eyed, his intensely black hair and slight accent were the only things suggesting his Chinese ancestry. Right then he was sticky with grease from the engine and dusty from the road. He glared at the part in his hand. "Found the problem and I think I'd better have a word with Mr. Andersen about it. I don't think this is good at all—"

Simon interrupted, knowing from experience just how long Robby could go on about things. "You know who Mr. Andersen is, right? The owner of Andersen Mining Corporation. I don't know that he'll talk to you."

"You think he'll talk to you?" Robby grinned to soften the retort. At Simon's startled expression, Robby added, "I know you've been trying to get a full-time job at the Sentinel for almost a year now. You're here, without Miss Trendle or her car, so this isn't official business. You're hoping for an interview, aren't you?"

Embarrassed, because he hadn't realized he was so obvious, Simon admitted it. "Miss Trendle did sanction my coming. If I can get a good story, she says she'll hire me full-time." Up until now he'd been limited to writing advertisements as a free-lancer when he wasn't driving Miss Trendle around town.

"Then let's go see if we can convince Mr. Snoot to talk to us." Robby held up the starter. "I might even have a hook for you." At Simon's confused expression, the mechanic tapped the device meaningfully. "My brother made a mess of things in there because he didn't notice this. It's been sabotaged. So what I want to know is if that Mr. Andersen fellow has an enemy who wants him dead."

Before Simon could answer, Robby crossed the street and entered the restaurant with an unexpected and uncharacteristic burst of speed.

They found four handsomely dressed older men sitting at a large table in a room off to the side of the main dining area. Mao, Uncle Ip's chief cook now that the old man was mostly retired, watched them expressionlessly, telling Simon just how annoyed the young chef was. Mao raised a brow at Robby, saying in Cantonese, "Don't sit down all dirty like that. You'll ruin the chairs."

"I wasn't planning on it," Robby answered in the same dialect, "Which one of those is Mr. Andersen?"

"What makes you think I know? I just cooked for them. They aren't interested in conversation."

Simon raised a brow. He knew Mao too well to think the chef hadn't paid attention. No matter how rich or poor, no matter how likeable or annoying, Mao stayed aware of his guests. "Because you're who you are."

Wryly, Mao admitted Simon was right. "But that lot don't talk when I'm around. I think they don't want me to overhear their business. Not that I'd understand much. My English still isn't very good."

"So?" Robby asked. "Which one is the big kahuna? The tall one? The one with the glasses—"

"None of them," Mao said before Robby could go on. "I'm not sure where Mr. Andersen went; I was in the kitchen cutting oranges when he left. Those four are Mr. Andersen's frogs—" The last word was in English and at Simon and Robby's confused expressions he tried again. "His flun-kies."

"His toadies?" Simon offered, unsurprised. He hadn't met any of the group when they'd visited the paper that morning, but Mr. Scanlon's comments about them suggested as much.

"Isn't that what I said? Oh, wait, did I use the wrong word again?" Seeing he had, Mao corrected himself. "Yes, toadies. Very much so."

Taking a handkerchief from his pocket and wiping his face and hands, Robby said, "Well, the only way we're going to find out where he is, is to ask."

Simon stopped Robby before he could march up to the group. "I may be better dressed for this," he said. Being of Chinese descent wasn't a point in his favor, but Robby looked the mechanic he was. There was no way a group of high-class businessmen would have the time of day for a man covered in grease and dust, carrying a block of metal and melted plastic.

Robby sighed. "You're probably right," he admitted. "You go on and I'll wait here for you."

Simon left Robby still talking and stepped through the round entryway into the side-room. Immediately the four men went silent, staring at him with unfriendly eyes. "Your pardon, sirs. I am looking for Mr. Alexander Andersen of Andersen Mining Corporation. Would he happen to be here?"

One, the oldest and obvious senior of the group curled his lip in a sneer. "Who are you and why do you want to know?"

Simon inclined his head politely. "I am Simon Lee, an associate of the Strikersport Sentinel. Miss Trendle asked me to request an interview with Mr. Andersen. Given, of course, that he's willing."

Another man laughed. "You're a reporter?" His tone held disbelief that a Chinese man could be anything of the sort, no matter how well dressed or well spoken.

"I am, sir." That was a bit of a fib, of course, given Simon had yet to earn the job, but he'd have no chance of getting an interview at all if they knew he was a chauffer who moonlighted as an advertisement writer for the Sentinel's radio station. "I do, of course, realize Mr. Andersen is here on vacation, but Miss Trendle understands that he's considering opening a factory here in Strikersport. She hoped he'd be willing to discuss his plans."

"Good luck with that," the oldest of the group muttered. "He won't even tell us."

Simon wasn't surprised. He'd researched the man before he headed up to Chinatown and Mr. Andersen was known for keeping his plans carefully secret until the moment he unveiled them. Which was probably why Miss Trendle hadn't sent one of her usual reporters on this job. Whether she expected Simon to fail or hoped he'd be unexpected and devious enough to get the story was a question he didn't want answered.

"I'm willing to try," Simon said. "But I can hardly do anything if I don't know where he is."

The same man glanced at his fellows and finally admitted, "We don't know either. He went to the gift shop next door about ten minutes ago, looking for his secretary, I think."

Simon sighed to himself and after a polite farewell, went to get Robby.

There was no one in the Jeen Loon when Simon and Robby entered, worrying Simon's companion. Small blame to him, either, since the store belonged to his mother. "Chou wouldn't leave the shop unattended," Robby said. "Besides, there's Hoshi's homework. She doesn't like working in the shop but she'd never just walk off."

Though unsure who Hoshi was, Simon guessed she must be one of the shop's employees, given the homework in question was sitting behind a counter near the door. "Pretty complicated math," he remarked, examining the neatly written pages. "And I didn't know any Japanese girls worked here."

"She's the daughter of a family friend. Half-Chinese, half-Japanese. Her father is a partner in the Jeen Loon aircraft company. He's a pilot. Her mother used to work for the American government, though now she's an official in a small kingdom near China." Robby's monologue continued as he drifted through the shop, skritching the head of the metal dragon statue sprawled on its back beside the radio. Helpfully, he added, "Aunt Hikaru is *Nisei*."

Though fascinating, Simon thought the story a distraction. "Let's wait on that until we've found her and Mr. Andersen. Is anything missing from the shop?" He looked around curiously, hard put to tell, given the sheer amount of knick-knacks the Jeen Loon sold. High priced knick-knacks, too, he thought, noticing a tag on a shelf of porcelain *shi shi* statues. Not one cost less than fifty dollars.

"I don't— Oh no. No. No. No." Robby rushed to the case in the middle of the room, where the pretty little statuettes purporting to be the Eight Immortals stood. They were an odd set, not at all like the Taoist Immortals

Simon had grown up with. He wondered just how the Monkey King had managed to find his way into this particular set of idols.

"What's wrong?" Simon watched Robby fumble with the lock.

"They're gone. They're all gone. They can't be gone." Robby babbled, obviously panicked. Before Simon could argue that there were still eight statues in the case, the man opened it up and swept his hand straight through the nearest one.

As the statue faded away, Simon came closer, watching Robby do the same to another statue. "What the hell? Where did they go?"

Robby looked at him. "I need to call my mother. You wait here. Don't touch anything. At all."

Before Simon could object, Robby ran to the back of the shop where his voice could be heard speaking a strange and unfamiliar dialect of Chinese. Whatever he was saying, Mrs. McLeod seemed to calm him down with little effort. No surprise, either. Simon had met the woman once and been impressed by her poise and self-possessed manner.

At last Robby came back, looking calmer, but still furious. "Simon, do you believe in magic?"

"I was at Miss Rosamund's charity ball last year, back when that gang of—whatever they were—attacked the party. I saw Tiger and Dragon fighting the others and that stranger suck fire into himself to save us all. I don't understand the half of what happened but I think it safe to say yes, I believe."

"Good. Because I'm going to need your help. There's an illusionist out there who stole our Eight Immortals statues and took Hoshi and Mr. Andersen. I have to find them."

Simon spread his hands. "I'm not sure what I can do, but—"

"The thing is, I don't see illusions. So I need you to show me where they are."

That made no sense to Simon whatsoever. "If this illusionist has hidden something with an illusion you can't see, isn't that a good thing?"

"Hoshi's an illusionist too and if I know her, she's marking the path they're taking her on. If so, I won't see the signs but you will."

Now Simon understood. He just hoped the sorcerer behind this mess didn't notice the girl's efforts.

Although a thief with illusionary skills could go any way they wanted, Robby decided to start their search in the back alley. Simon wasn't so sure, mostly because the back alleys of the district were a tangled maze only the most experienced could navigate. He'd have thought a thief would want to get out of Chinatown quickly. Still, Robby turned out to be right. The very first thing Simon saw when they exited the building was a pretty little star glittering in mid-air. It was a lovely thing and only visible from the exact right angle.

Scanning the alley, Simon walked sideways, then bent backwards so he could see the next star. "She's not making this easy," he muttered, describing what he saw for Robby's sake.

"She's probably trying to keep her illusion hidden from her captor. She made the first one obvious so we can find it, luckily. She's pretty smart that way."

Following the sparkles, Simon grew more and more impressed with Hoshi's abilities. It wasn't just her ability to create the things, but her ability to hide them in ways that grew ever more devious the further they went. Sometimes the stars appeared just above his head, visible at only one angle. Sometimes they were hidden against a sign. Even more deviously, she'd begun leaving them a message as she went, placing her stars atop specific words.

It was Robby who realized what she was saying. "Five men, two sorcerers. Caution advised," he said. "As if I wasn't going to be careful?"

Simon shrugged at the complaint. "Better forewarned, surely," he pointed out.

"Even so." Robby grumbled. "I know I talk too much and I move too slow, but I'm not stupid."

A thought occurred to Simon as they turned the corner and found themselves on one of the main streets. "Maybe so, but would she be expecting you? Or doesn't she know you don't see illusions?"

Robby contemplated the question as they continued back towards the center of Chinatown. "She does know," he admitted. "You could be right. She might have expected Chou. In fact, she probably did. He can be a bit distractible."

By this time they were almost to *Chiming* Temple. It was another of those oddities about Strikersport's Chinatown. Grandly decorated, it almost seemed to be more for show than a place of actual worship. Oh, it was used, but something about the elegant gold designs on the walls and the central pagoda rising tall above the city was overdone, grandiose in a manner that didn't fit with the quiet ways of Chinatown's inhabitants.

Someday Simon might ask about this place's history. Not yet, though, because despite being Chinese himself, he was an outsider among these people. They had a distinct and peculiar culture that bore only a passing resemblance to the one he'd grown up in. Which, when he thought about it, came as no surprise. It wasn't as if the Chinese—American born or not—were one people with the exact same backgrounds and exact same traditions. Strikersport's Chinese population was just a little more different than the rest.

Hoshi's stars led them straight up the temple steps, a series of glittering sparkles set into the eyes of the dragons guarding the path. The last one gleamed gold within a paper lantern hanging right above the doorway. "In here?" Robby said, with a faint note of anger in his voice.

Simon wasn't best pleased, either. He liked to think of himself as a modern man, free of the old superstitions, but he'd been properly brought up and the idea of someone using a temple for criminal purposes was infuriating.

Lacking any other direction, they entered the temple and stopped in the large open chamber in the middle. There was a reclining Buddha, large but not as big as the one in Thailand, in the center, a porcelain—no, marble—statue of a *shi shi* cub curled in the palm of his huge hand.

A skinny young man wearing a hooded saffron robe sat before the Buddha, murmuring soft and familiar prayers. He ignored their entry, entirely focused on what he was doing. Robby glanced at him, then made a questioning gesture at Simon, who searched around the temple for Hoshi's little stars. He frowned, unable to see anything. Had they lost the trail or had Hoshi's efforts been noticed? If the latter, perhaps this was was a false trail, lain by the other illusionist to confuse pursuit?

Simon was about to draw Robby back, to tell him his suspicions, but when he turned, he saw one of the statues against the wall—the God of War, he thought—suddenly begin to move. More statues broke free of their bases and he stared in horror. "Is—is that an illusion too?"

Spinning to look where Simon pointed, Robby snarled under his breath. "No. It's a different sorcerer's work. We'd better get out of here."

They backed up, trying to find a clear path, and were slowly forced towards the spot where the priest sat, praying quietly. Pushed right up against the rail, with the statues slowly closing in, Simon stared at the man and demanded. "How can he ignore all this?"

"I don't think he is," Robby answered. "I think—" Whatever it was

Robby thought became a moot point a moment later, as the floor beneath Simon suddenly disappeared. Flailing wildly in search of a handhold, Simon caught a better glimpse of the priest's face beneath his hood. He was startled to see the man was Caucasian, with red eyebrows and bright blue eyes.

The priest smiled at Simon, one hand raised in mocking benediction, his eyes strangely empty. Then Simon dropped into darkness.

Simon wasn't sure how long it was before he roused. "Robby? Robby, are you all right?"

Another voice, gruff and unfamiliar, spoke. "I sent young master McLeod for help. You'll have to make do with me." A light sparked at the tips of five sharp claws and lit up a slender stick like a lightbulb. Blinking, Simon realized he was laying on the floor of a pit, a tall man in a hooded black longcoat standing nearby, peering upwards into the darkness. He was a familiar figure, the red-masked man they called Tiger.

Refusing to point out the obvious, Simon demanded, "I wasn't unconscious that long, was I? Why didn't he wake me up?"

"Possibly he couldn't. Possibly he felt you were safer here." Tiger turned to look at Simon. "Possibly he felt I'd be better at protecting you than he was."

Though he would have liked to argue the point, Robby wasn't there for Simon to argue with. Instead, he asked, "How did you get here, then?"

"Much the same way you did. I dropped." Tiger chuckled. "Of course, our captors forget that I'm never entirely alone."

"Dragon, you mean?"

"Dragon is otherwise engaged, or so I understand." Shrugging off the question, Tiger assisted Simon to his feet. "I mean Yuan."

"Empress Yuan?" Simon asked, frowning. "Or—"

"My Beauty," Tiger told him. "Sorry, my Chinese has a Khaitan accent. Hei Yuan, Black Beauty. My motorcycle."

Khaitan was a myth, or so Simon thought, but he didn't argue the point. Not when he'd just followed a trail of illusionary stars into a trap guarded by several dozen walking statues. "Your motorcycle can get down here, wherever here is?"

"She can get anywhere I need her to." Tiger walked around the small pit and stopped at a door. "However, we might want to try this first. Robby mentioned thieves and an abduction, I believe, and they may be using this cellar as a hideout."

Though the theft at the Jeen Loon had nothing to do with Tiger, Simon didn't argue the point. Instead he said, "There's a girl—"

"Hoshi. I know. And a man named Andersen. If you want to come with me, I won't stop you."

Having gone through everything he had so far, with a story that might be even better than the one he'd been assigned in the offing, what could Simon do but agree?

The door was locked, but Tiger easily broke it down. That, however, led them straight into the arms of a small gang of toughs. All Chinese, Simon noted, ducking blows and hoping his limited martial arts training would keep him safe. He'd mostly learned for his father's sake and he didn't pretend to be very good at it.

"Who are these people?" Tiger demanded, executing a spinning kick that knocked two of their attackers down at once. "They're not from around here."

Looking at the toughs, Simon didn't know how Tiger could be so sure. They were all of Chinese descent and dressed in non-descript grey uniforms. They wore white bandanas around their left biceps with an indecipherable *hanzi* character on it; their Tong affiliation, Simon guessed. Some were thin, some big and muscular, but they looked like they belonged together. "You know every gang member in Chinatown, I take it?"

"Well, actually, I do," Tiger admitted. "We've even butted heads a few times."

Simon didn't doubt that. There were rumored to be several small tongs in Chinatown, one for each of the four quarters and another, larger one that kept the other four in order. "If you say so."

Tiger ran up the wall, flipped and swung a peculiar weapon formed of a series of flat metal bars, knocking another gang member to the ground. Then he tore a bandana from another man's arm as he passed, tossing the cloth to Simon. "I do. There's no centipede Tong around here. Not unless someone's getting uppity."

The character on the bandana was indeed centipede and Simon tried to remember why the name seemed familiar. At the same time he let loose with a series of rapid punches that would have made his father proud. Or, would have until he managed to fumble and trip over his own two feet trying to get out of the way of another attacker. He took a sharp blow to the side of his head and was sent reeling straight into Tiger.

Fortunately, the masked man paid better attention than Simon. He caught him by the arm and steadied him.

"Sorry," Simon said, desperately embarrassed.

"Everyone has bad days," Tiger said as he knocked Simon's last attacker down. "You've never been in a real fight before."

Guessing his limited skill showed his equally limited training, Simon agreed. "My father ran a club back in New York."

"So I've heard." Tiger checked their opponents and made sure they were all unconscious. Before Simon could ask how the man knew anything about him, he added curtly, "Tie them up, then let's go."

Dealing with their attackers was the work of a few minutes and they were soon headed down the hall. There weren't any more little stars to guide them but this was the only path, so it didn't matter. Simon looked around, nervously expecting trouble and was surprised when no one attacked. Did that mean the fight was finished?

Then they stepped into a larger room at the end of the hall and Simon knew it wasn't. A broad faced older man in his fifties stood atop a dais at the far end of the room. He was oddly dressed, wearing robes more suited to a historical drama—Cases of Judge Bao, perhaps—than modern day California. His dark hair was greying and his eyes were narrowed in a way that made Simon wonder if he needed glasses.

There was a gold throne behind the man, a dragon curled around its base and coming up over its back. Two figures were sprawled in front of it, a young girl and a man. They were both unconscious and both—surely— the ones Simon and Robby had been looking for.

Ordinarily, the room would have been a gorgeous sight, with curtains of red silk and paper lanterns painted with ornate flowers. The beauty, however, was hidden away by thousands, no, millions, of centipedes, crawling over the walls and ceiling.

"It had to be centipedes," Tiger muttered. "I hate centipedes."

"THERE'S NO CENTIPEDE TONG AROUND HERE."

"There's an illusionist around. Maybe—"

Tiger crushed one, gloved hand sparking as he struck. "No. These are real. Unfortunately." He continued forward, Simon close behind.

The man waiting for them smiled triumphantly, though Simon thought there was a faint uncertainty in his manner, as if things weren't going quite his way. "Welcome, Tiger," he said in Cantonese. "I knew I'd have to deal with you sooner or later. But where is Dragon? I was so looking forward to seeing her again."

Tiger cocked his head. "Sorry. Do I know you?"

A look of pure fury crossed the man's face. "You—you dare ask? You dare pretend you don't know who I am? You, the same man who interfered with my plans at every turn in Canton? You who got me arrested in Nanjing and sent to the Mongolian desert?"

As the man's diatribe continued, describing Tiger's ancestry, hygiene and general manners, Tiger listened with an air of distant interest. When the tide of insults ebbed, he finally said, "Sorry. Just doesn't ring a bell. Must have been a different Tiger."

Fury suffused the stranger's face and Simon couldn't help interjecting, "I thought Dragon was a man, anyway."

"He is," Tiger agreed. "Last I saw him, at least. You never know with Dragon." He drew an object from his sleeve and tossed it to the ground. Whatever it was exploded in a small burst of light and smoke, sending the centipedes skittering away in terror. Immediately Tiger rolled forward, rushing the dais.

Simon followed, unsure how to help. Stamp on those damned bugs, he supposed, but not much else. He was just coming up behind Tiger when a woman rushed into the room from the other direction. Her appearance made Tiger start and while his expression was impossible to read beneath the mask, Simon thought she frightened him.

"WUGONG," the newcomer shouted. "That girl stole the idols!"

"What?" The man, who must have been Wugong, turned to look back at the girl on the floor. "Are you out of your mind? She's right there."

The two argued and Simon narrowed his eyes, looking more closely at the girl himself. Hoshi was supposed to be an illusionist. What if she'd used her talent to create a false image of herself? Knowing better than to let the enemy realize, he touched Tiger on the shoulder lightly and pointed to Hoshi's apparent form, shaking his head ever so slightly. "Illusion," he mouthed, when Tiger looked at him. "I think."

Tiger looked thoughtfully at the dais for a moment and grinned.

Leaping forward, he caught Mr. Andersen up and tossed the man over his shoulder, ignoring muffled complaints. Then he rushed for the same door the woman had come through and Simon followed as fast as his legs could carry him.

Wugong's indignant yells echoed up the stairwell, along with hurrying footsteps. A monster appeared to block their path, a twisted form of a man dressed in a scholar's robe, his gaping mouth bloody and filled with twisted fangs as he hopped down the steps at them.

When Simon stumbled to a halt, unabashedly terrified by the sight of the *jiangshi*, Tiger said, "Don't stop. Whatever you see, whatever you think you see, just run."

Realizing Tiger was right, because Hoshi wasn't the only illusionist they were dealing with, Simon ran again, straight through the figure. Flames were next, but they had no heat and Simon ignored them readily. The pack of hyenas were from a different continent and no one could be intimidated by a set of chilly shadows that did nothing more than lean lazily against the walls of the stairway.

"That one doesn't belong here," Tiger muttered as they passed. "But I'll take all the help I can get."

Simon had no idea what the masked man meant, but by then they'd reached the top of the stairs and returned to the temple floor. A girl's voice called, "Look out, Tiger!" just as one of those walking statues swung a wooden fist at both him and Simon.

Evading the attack as quickly as his reflexes allowed, Simon realized a fight had broken out during their absence. A girl was leaping from one pair of wooden shoulders to another, a torn bag slung over her shoulder. A half dozen poorly dressed thugs tried to catch her, but a pair of police officers were blocking their path. Simon recognized the latter as Maloney and his newest partner, a fellow named Gilly Kenneth. Maloney was wailing on one of the men and Gilly was quietly and patiently evading the blows of one of the statues. For some reason, the thing was smoldering, as if it were burning from the inside out.

"Well this is unexpected," Tiger said, dodging past a statue to join Simon. "Here. You keep an eye on Andersen. I'll help Hoshi." He didn't give Simon a chance to object, setting the man in a corner before joining the girl in her gymnastics atop the statues.

Mr. Andersen squirmed around in his bonds, clearly furious, and Simon put a hand on the man's gag. "I'll free you," he said. "But you have to be quiet. Don't draw attention to yourself."

To Simon's complete surprise, Andersen actually went silent, laying still and glaring at Simon with hot fury. Cautiously, Simon removed the gag and continued to be surprised when all Andersen said was, "I swear, heads will roll for this."

As long as those heads were ones that actually deserved it, Simon didn't really care. He undid the man's bonds carefully. "I'd try to get you out of here, but I don't see a clear path to the exit. We'll have to wait."

Lips pursed, Andersen nodded and Simon was relieved not to have that argument on his hands. He looked around, trying to think if there was something he could do. He didn't know who the toughs were, except— not being Chinese—they were obviously outsiders; thieves who must have thought to rob the temple while Chinatown was busy getting ready for the festival. There were only a few, though, and Maloney and his partner seemed to have matters in hand.

As for the statues themselves, there was no way Simon could do anything to stop them. Accepting the existence of magic didn't tell him how to fight it. Then he noticed the priest still sitting there, serene amid the chaos, seeming to pray, and remembered the way the fellow had smirked. Was he with the pair Simon and Tiger had met downstairs?

Reminded of the other two, Simon glanced back the way they came. To his surprise, neither Wugong, nor his companion appeared, though they'd not been far behind Simon and Tiger earlier. There were no more illusions, either, except for the black shadows roiling around the stairwell, blocking it entirely. Did that mean the illusionist couldn't attack them, here in the temple itself?

One of those shadows snaked its way towards Simon and he couldn't help jerking back. A chill swept over him and a voice whispered in his ear. "Some sorcereries cannot outlast their sorcerer."

A man's hand tried to push past the shadows in the stairway and the voice added, "Sorry. We'd help more, but that one's keeping us busy." The shadowy serpent returned to its source and from somewhere beneath the swirling darkness, Simon heard curses in Cantonese.

Guessing he'd been given the closest thing to help he was going to get, Simon looked back at the fight. The biggest problem was those statues and now he was certain the priest controlled them. Thinking hard about what he'd been told, Simon searched around and found a wooden candleholder. Cautiously, he picked it up and snuck behind the priest. Then, with an apologetic look to the Buddha for his unseemly behavior, he knocked the man out.

For a moment, Simon wasn't sure if he'd guessed rightly. The statues were still moving, still trying to get their hands on the others. Then they slowed, slowed some more, until they dropped to the floor, crashing down with enough force to splinter the wood.

The toughs stared around, realized they were alone, and started to make a run for it. Except Officer Kenneth grabbed one and Tiger another, dragging them back towards the center of the room. At the same time, Wugong and his partner stumbled out of the shadows, both cursing and sputtering furiously. "I'm not done with you, Tiger."

"Yes, you are," the shadows said, coming together into a single jet black shape like a coiled serpent. "You're outnumbered, little bug, and the earth's own fire awaits you if you stay."

Simon wasn't sure what the shadows meant, but the threat had the desired effect. Wugong and his companion set off running.

The shadowy serpent turned its attention on the rest of them and Tiger stepped forward, bowing politely. "Your help was most appreciated, ancient one." He lifted his head and added, "But you should not be here and this one is most curious as to the reason we are graced with your presence."

The flowery court language made the serpent laugh. "Save your pretty words for the Elder Four, boy. As for why we're here, blame the one behind you."

As Maloney spluttered at the accusation, Hoshi said, "He thought I was one of the thieves and tried to take the bag from me. It tore it open and four of the idols fell out. They—broke." Sounding offended, she added, "I did tell him I work at the Jeen Loon, too."

Tiger turned on the officer, "Maloney, are you ever going to learn to leave well enough alone?"

With a chuckle, Officer Kenneth said, "Probably not." That elicited a glare from Maloney and the younger officer added, with a nervous glance for the serpent, "For what it's worth, it wouldn't be a problem at all if it was just the statues breaking."

"Indeed. A brief summoning indeed, child of fire," the serpent said, inclining its huge head to the officer. "But a broken *daitsushi*, what some would call a riftstone, has been roused. Worse, it is the Feast of Hungry Ghosts in Khaitan and the barrier between worlds is thin and growing thinner. The damage has been done and all the Younger Four can do is try to hold the ramparts. Stopping those who would misuse the power is up to you and that nuisance kinsman of yours, young Tiger."

With that, the serpent's shadows expanded, filling the room with their chill dark. Then both they and Tiger were gone.

Once things settled, Simon hurried back to Mr. Andersen. The man was obviously furious over the whole affair but, fortunately for Simon, directed his anger at the one who'd kidnapped him. "I promise, I will have that man's head on a platter. How dare he interfere with me? And where the devil is Rogers?"

Behind Simon, Hoshi was telling Maloney, "Wugong's companion tricked me into thinking the case was empty. I opened it, wishing to verify what I saw and they grabbed me. Mr. Andersen was just entering the store and they took him as well, to keep me in line. Otherwise they would have had a fight. I know my uncle's little ways."

Simon glanced over his shoulder as he helped Mr. Andersen to his feet. "Uncle?"

"Yes. Wugong was disinherited, but he was my father's older brother." Hoshi waved off the question. "That's for later. The point is, he wanted the statues."

"What about that lot?" Maloney demanded, pointing at the two men Officer Kenneth held in a surprisingly powerful grip. "I've never seen them around here before."

"How should I know?" Hoshi shrugged. "They just showed up out of nowhere."

Officer Kenneth turned one of his prisoners to face him and patted the frightened man's cheek. "Now, now. I'm not going to hurt you. That'd be police brutality."

"I'll talk. I'll talk. They're not paying me enough for this!" To Simon's surprise, the man's accent had a distinct East Coast sound. A true outsider, then, which might explain why he'd been fool enough to try something in Strikersport's Chinatown.

"Well?"

"Uh—what you want to know? Only I don't know much. the boss doesn't tell us schmucks nothing."

"The boss doesn't tell us schmucks anything," Officer Kenneth corrected

"This isn't time for a grammar lesson, Kenneth!" Maloney snapped.

"Nonsense, there's always time for a grammar lesson." The officer returned his attention to his prisoner. "Where's your boss, then?"

"Over in the southeast section, taking care of another job. That's all I know."

By this time Simon had finished with Mr. Andersen. From the man's expression, it was obvious he was ready to lop some heads off, starting with those present. No doubt he'd have set into the two officers, but that was when Robby came running into the building, accompanied by a dozen of Boss Chang's best men. To Simon's surprise, Boss Chang himself was right behind Robby, sauntering along as if out for a stroll.

"Do something about this mess," Chang ordered. As his men began cleaning up, the old man approached Mr. Andersen. "I am most apologetic. I had not heard that a man of your caliber was gracing my small enclave. Had I not met your lovely wife just a short while ago, I still would not know. I am most terribly sorry that you have received such brutal treatment at the hands of the thugs and thieves who—most unfortunately—find their way into even the most peaceful of places."

"You are—" Mr. Andersen began, staring at the ill-dressed old man with an expression of disbelief.

"I am Cheh Chang, the Mayor of this little place and the head of Jeen Loon Enterprises. I believe you were hoping to meet with me regarding some imported antiquities from China? Perhaps you would care to join me to discuss your thoughts over a cup of tea?"

Simon deeply admired Boss Chang's smooth and easy way of pouring oil over Mr. Andersen's troubled waters. It worked, too, for Mr. Andersen brushed himself off and said, "I was expecting to meet with you later today, but this is much better. All right."

Simon noted Hoshi was taking the bag of idols, at least those remaining, back to the Jeen Loon. At the same time, Mr. Chang's men were handling the cleanup and the two policemen had already gone off, after the gang's boss, no doubt. Without hesitation, he stepped forward. "Mr. Andersen? I apologize for interrupting but—"

"What is it, boy? Are you expecting a reward?" Mr. Andersen pulled out a wallet, obviously intending to pay Simon off.

Before the man could open the thing, Simon raised a hand to stop him. "If you wish to reward me, sir," he said politely, "perhaps you would be willing to allow me an interview?"

After all, while the adventure had been fascinating and certainly newsworthy, Simon had an assignment and he intended to complete it.

Chapter Three
Krane Winery has Weekly Garden Parties and Wine Tasting

"Well, that was an interesting turn of events."

Maloney glared straight ahead.

"I certainly couldn't have predicted it."

"Hmph."

"Except, of course, I did try to warn you."

Maloney muttered.

"I'm sorry, sir. I didn't quite get that."

"I said, 'The hell you did.'"

"Begging your pardon, boss man, but I distinctly remember saying, 'This is a temple, it's almost time for the Feast of Hungry Ghosts, and I feel the Old Powers stirring. Be careful not to offend them.'"

"And how is keeping a snooty little miss from running off with a bag of stolen goods offending any old powers?"

Gilly Kenneth, AKA Uncle Gilly, AKA Old Smokey, AKA one small and broken off shard of the nearly forgotten *unhcegila* monster turned—mostly—human, grinned broadly. As a former piece of chaos, summoned and shaped by human fear and belief, situations like this naturally amused him. "She told you she worked for the Jeen Loon. You might have believed her, instead of trying to take her bag away like she was a naughty little girl in need of a spanking."

"She was, though. If she'd just handed it over like I told her—"

"If you'd listened to me trying to warn you—"

"Look, just shut up and drive. We have to report to Michaels and I'm trying to think of what to say."

"Right you are, boss man." Focusing on his driving, the former monster turned rookie cop considered the incident thoughtfully. The trouble was, while he was mentally quite old, his memories of the days when he'd been the sum of his first people's fears, or even the terror of Strikersport's back alleys were fading. Oh, he would never fully forget being a monster, but his transformation from a thing of fear and dread to a physical being meant his concerns were driven by fragile and all too mortal flesh.

The one memory he did retain, however, was the knowledge that belief and faith shaped the Gods' power. Back in his early existence, the date would have had little to no significance. The peoples whose minds and fears had created him didn't regard it as important. The people of Strikersport's Chinatown, however, did. And that, in turn, meant the Feast of Hungry Ghosts carried a great deal of significance in this place and time.

Maloney's righteous insistence that the young lady from the Jeen Loon hand over the goods so he could take them down to the police station had resulted in minor disaster. At least Gilly hoped it was a minor disaster. The deities those idols represented belonged to a tiny and God-haunted kingdom sitting outside human reality. In most places, they'd have no connection to this world. Strikersport was another story altogether. The inhabitants of the local Chinatown were members of a tribe who still worshipped those old and quirky powers.

Of course, the real trouble was the sorcerer who'd been summoning the energies of the rift—the void outside the worlds—at the same time. Gilly still wasn't sure what the man was thinking, given he was thinking at all, but being partially connected to the rift himself, he'd sensed the rising danger and been helpless to prevent it.

In a way, breaking those statues might have been better for all concerned. It'd redirected some of the rift energies and weakened the sorcerer's spell. That it'd given the old Gods of far-off Khaitan a foothold in the human world was something they'd all have to deal with now.

It was fortunate the broken statues were the lesser of Khaitan's eight Gods, the weaker four whose mortal forms could walk the Earth without harming it. If the other four found their way into the physical world—well, even an old former monster of chaos could be terrified at the prospect. Amused, but also terrified. Meng Huang Hsiang and Shen Lung weren't too bad, but their parents, the Queen Mother of the South and the King Father of the North were old and dangerous beings one crossed at one's peril.

Driving through Strikersport, Gilly contemplated the last hour or so thoughtfully. They'd been called to the Jeen Loon by some businessmen who'd been eating at Uncle Ip's. A gang of thugs had apparently tried to break into the shop and been chased up Chinatown's main street by some of the district's local protectors.

Ordinarily, Maloney left well-enough alone in Chinatown. Though officially part of Strikersport, its inhabitants didn't cooperate with outsiders, especially white outsiders. Hell, they didn't cooperate with Gilly and he didn't look white at all to most people. But Maloney had heard that the businessmen's boss was some bigwig named Andersen and wanted to show he was on the ball. Gilly, fond of mischief as he was, hadn't discouraged his superior officer; now he wished he had.

The fight in the temple had resulted in Maloney's mistake. Gilly had felt the power when the things shattered and seen what no one else had; four brightly shining forms rise from the shards. A monkey, an eagle, a serpent and a strange mask like being. All but the serpent had scattered to parts unknown, as if searching for something.

Unaware of the result of his interference, Maloney had insisted on going off after the thugs' boss, rather than stay where he was to explain things to Cheh Chang. That had led to the fight between one of Chinatown's tongs—the Tofu Water Gang—and the rescue of Mr. Andersen's wife from the gang who'd kidnapped her. Not that they'd much to do with the rescue; that had been Dragon and Miss Frazier's doing.

Gilly had a feeling something had happened there, too. There'd been a scent of magic and mythic power in the air that had had nothing whatsoever to do with Dragon. Somehow, he suspected the repercussions of Maloney's actions were resonating through the town and making themselves known all over the place. The next few hours were going to be interesting, in the proverbial Chinese sense.

By this time he and Maloney had arrived at the police station and parked. It surprised Gilly a little to realize he'd done so automatically, barely aware of having turned into the parking lot. He wasn't human, even retained certain aspects of his old abilities, but it seemed he was becoming more and more settled in his role. Just as well, he supposed. Going back to his old ways was occasionally tempting but not as entertaining.

"Stop daydreaming, Kenneth," Maloney snapped. "We'd better go tell Michaels what happened."

Up in Chief Michaels' office, Gilly happily left Maloney the task of explaining everything. Michaels wasn't best pleased by the prospect of dealing with Mr. and Mrs. Andersen's complaints over their experiences but he was even less pleased at the rest of Maloney's tale. "You did what?"

"I didn't do it my own self," Maloney complained. "It was an accident, it was. That's all."

"An accident Gilly thinks has released some weird old Gods on Strikersport?" Michaels asked, obviously trying to remain calm.

Gilly couldn't resist poking his long nose in. "Now I wouldn't say released. That implies they were imprisoned in the first place. It's just that they don't usually come around here. Well, except for Meng Huang Hsiang, and he's an odd duck."

A sudden chill went up Gilly's spine and he shuddered. He probably shouldn't have used that name. The mad Dream God of Khaitan approved of him, but the Mad One was still a God and Gilly—though no longer a monster—always felt nervous around him. Fortunately, the God didn't attempt to communicate, though Gilly was pretty sure he had his attention.

"What is it?" Michaels demanded. "More trouble?"

"No. Not yet." Gilly sighed. "We'll have to see." He wondered if he should mention the rift energies and decided not. There wasn't much Michaels could do about it. Besides, Gilly had no idea where the damned thing was. That 'priest' had run off with it before anyone had noticed and there was no need to add to Michaels' worries.

"So what does this business mean? Who are those four Gods you're talking about and what are they likely to do, here in Strikersport?"

Gilly shrugged. "Why ask me?"

"Because you're the closest thing I have to an expert in the supernatural."

While that was true, it didn't mean Gilly was going to be much, if any, use. "I was a monster. Emphasis on was. Monsters generally only know enough to fulfill the requirements of their nature. While I'll admit to having a bit more knowledge than that, I'm still no expert."

"You're going to have to do, though. I'm not bothering Mrs. McLeod with this when it's my own men who managed to cause the trouble. At least, not until I have to."

Gilly didn't blame the Chief. Mudan McLeod would have choice words for everyone involved and like Michaels, he'd prefer them aimed at pretty much anyone but himself. With a sigh, he said, "I might have a theory. It may not be a good one."

"Let me be the judge of that."

"I suspect there are a few too many fingers stirring the pot. That priest in the temple was up to no good. Looking to cash in on the energies of the festival, I think, and biting off more than he could chew. He didn't plan to pull in those four; they just took advantage of the chance. Then there are those thugs—the ones who were most definitely not from Chinatown. Not sure where their place is in all this but from what the one said, they were looking for those statues too."

Michaels considered the last. "Back before you—became mortal—that Voice fellow was trying to get hold of the one statue so he could use it to control—the God it represents. Could this gang's boss have a similar idea?"

"I have no idea, frankly." Gilly thought about what the thugs had said. "At a guess, I'd say they know the things are valuable. Whether that's because they're part of a significant set of—what's the term—*objet d'art*—or because the Gods they represent can be contacted through them, that's out of my field. If the latter, they haven't a chance of controlling even the weakest of that lot."

Michaels sighed. "I'll talk to Jarvis about this. He'll need to know the details."

"Good idea." William Jarvis had been Maloney's partner before Gilly, but Michaels had set him the job of investigating situations like this one. Sooner or later Gilly would be working with Jarvis, too, but there was no way Michaels could justify sticking a rookie cop on a specialized and elite task-force. As for Maloney, the man was a natural beat-cop, no two ways about it.

Michaels eyed Maloney, adding, "In the meantime, I want the two of you out of trouble. We've been asked to provide security for the soiree up at the winery this afternoon. You two go handle that."

Before Maloney could protest, Gilly grinned. "Oh, goody! A wine-tasting. I'll enjoy that." He hustled his superior officer out of Michaels' office before the police chief could remember that he was—in essence—sending a wolf to guard the sheep.

Because if there was anything Gilly still retained from his days as a monster, it was his deep and abiding fondness for alcohol. Admittedly, he preferred the rotgut whiskey his good friend Crogan served at Barton's to the prissy stuff they made up at the Krane vineyard.

Still, any port in a storm, after all.

"You will need to wear these."

The Krane family's butler; their fifth since Old Timothy had bit the dust, or rather an old and too solid table, eyed Gilly and Maloney with a dour expression as he held out two black suits. Jones was a short, heavyset fellow with a snooty nose and the frustrated air of one who'd had quite enough. Gilly couldn't blame him. Old Timothy had spoiled his charges outrageously. Now his successors were left dealing with three adults who expected to be catered to like children.

As if thinking of the Kranes summoned them, Mrs. Krane appeared at the door to the butler's office to demand, "The party will be beginning soon and the caterer has barely gotten started." Her son echoed his mother's words, as if Jones were quite deaf and needed extra prodding to attend to their requirements.

"I apologize, ma'am. I will speak with Mrs. McLeod immediately." As soon as the two Kranes had left, Jones glared at Maloney and Gilly, daring them to comment. "You two get changed and go to the garden. Don't touch anything, don't eat anything and don't drink anything, understood?"

Once the butler was gone, Maloney muttered, "This is Michaels' way of getting back at me."

"I thought I was Michaels' way of getting back at you," Gilly answered, changing into the suit he'd been given as quickly as he could. "Besides, if Mrs. McLeod is here, it's probably his idea of getting even with me, too."

Maloney snorted at the idea. "She's a powerful—whatever it is she is— but you're not a monster anymore. Why are you so afraid of her?"

Gilly eyed his superior officer dourly. "Would you like to tell her what happened at the Jeen Loon then? I'm sure she'd love to hear all about it. Given she doesn't already know."

"Ah—No. I think I'll be passing on that idea." Maloney struggled with his tie, forcing Gilly to come over to assist him. "I'm not wanting to find out what she'll say when she hears about those statues."

"What statues?" a voice said from the doorway and Gilly turned to see the third member of the Krane family standing there. She was elegantly dressed in dark gold for a proper garden party, her big and faithful wolf-hound Boopsie beside her, wearing a matching collar. "Oh, it's you, Officer Kenneth. I didn't think mother would have invited you, after what you said to her the other night." She sipped at the wine in her glass, a deep red drink whose scent Gilly recognized immediately.

"She didn't invite me," Gilly said, putting the final touches on Maloney's tie. Then he took the glass from Rosamund, draining it before she could object. "You don't really think putting cranberry juice in Barton's finest will hide the fact you're drinking it again when you know what it does to you?"

Rosamund Krane glared at him and took the glass back. "Boopsie. He's a mean man. Bite him for me."

As always when Rosamund gave her beloved pet that order, the dog looked from her to Gilly and, with a sigh, lay down on the floor beside his mistress. "You're a terrible guard dog, Boopsie. You tell him to stop taking my drink away."

"Boopsie knows what I know," Gilly answered, amused by the young woman's temper and the dog's disinterest in obeying her order, "That you drink too much. Stop it, before you wind up as useless and worthless as that toad masquerading as your brother."

"My brother is not a toad!"

"True. That was an insult to toads."

Gilly's inevitable response had the desired effect and Rosamund quite obviously had to fight back a giggle. Then she composed herself. "I don't like our wine and I don't know why you keep picking on me."

"You don't have to drink your family's wine if you don't like it. You haven't had a good pressing for decades, anyway. As for why I pick on you? Someone has to do it, before you drink yourself into an early grave or give yourself a fit of apoplexy from that temper of yours."

Rosamund tightened her lips but didn't argue the point anymore. "I asked Jones if anything needed done and he suggested I show you two where the garden is. So follow me and I'll do just that."

The Krane Winery's garden was an elegant little affair that required far more care and tending than most. Someone—Mrs. Krane, most likely—had insisted on plants unsuited to Northern California and a small army of gardeners spent most of their time keeping the delicate flowers alive despite their inclination to wilt and die. It was an impressive feat, even to Gilly's eyes.

"You two know what you're supposed to do, right?" Rosamund demanded, once they'd entered the grounds.

Maloney and Gilly's only job was to ensure no uninvited guests found their way into the party, an easy task given it hadn't even started yet. So far, the only people other than themselves were Mrs. McLeod's catering service. They ignored the newcomers, busy preparing an elaborate buffet of rich tidbits to accompany the winery's latest vintage.

"We know well enough," Maloney said before Gilly could open his mouth. "You just run right along now, Miss Krane. We'll be fine."

Rosamund sniffed. "I'll believe that when I see it," she told them both, walking away with Boopsie at her side. Gilly turned away to look out at the ocean to their west, but he could sense Rosamund's eyes on him as she left and knew she'd paused to glance their way. He smirked to himself, refus-

" YOU TWO KNOW WHAT YOU'RE GOING TO DO, RIGHT ? "

ing to turn. Some things were better kept private.

"Why do you pick on her, anyway?" Maloney asked, once they seemed safely alone again.

"Because it pleases me to do so." Gilly scanned the sky. Why did he have such an odd feeling? The business back in Chinatown ought to have stayed in Chinatown. Yet he felt a quiver in the flow of the world's energies, a faint tremble that boded something. Whether good or ill, he couldn't say.

"'Pleases you to do so'? What kind of answer is that, then? What's pleasing about getting that spoiled brat all het up and angry with you? And why do you care if she drinks herself into an early grave? You're not her father. Or her mother, rather, given Mr. Krane's dead, God rest his soul."

Gilly wasn't at all sure Jack Krane's soul was anywhere near resting in peace. He didn't say so, however, knowing how Maloney felt about such things. "Well, no. Given no one around her but me seems to care she's destroying all her potential—"

Maloney snorted. "Potential? Her?"

"Potential. Her," Gilly agreed equably. "Put in the right place, with the right teaching, there's a great deal Rosie could have done with all her wealth and influence. Instead she's a frustrated prima donna, looking for attention from everyone and getting it in the worst way. Instead she's hiding from an empty life, full of everything she wants and nothing she needs."

Mrs. McLeod spoke behind Gilly, "She is organized, skilled at finding a person's—desires—and when she wishes, she can be quite kind. But, as you say, she drinks too much."

Startled, because Mrs. McLeod was one of the few people who could sneak up on him, Gilly turned and stared at her. She was simply dressed in dark grey western clothes, her still-dark hair pulled back in a tight ponytail and her lips only faintly tinted. The right clothes for the right job, Gilly thought. Mudan McLeod had an impressive aura of self-possession even without the elaborate robes she wore as a priestess of Meng Huang Hsiang.

The lady eyed Gilly thoughtfully. "Why is it I sense guilt, Old One?" she asked. "More guilt than usual, that is."

It was Maloney who swallowed and said, "It wouldn't be his fault, ma'am. What happened over in Chinatown, that is. Truth is, I'm the one caused the trouble."

As calmly as he possibly could, Gilly pointed out, "You might have held your tongue a bit longer, Maloney. She didn't know about that mess until you opened your big mouth."

"She'll find out soon enough, though," Maloney told him with admirable logic. "Might as well come clean."

With a smile that promised trouble later, Mrs. McLeod said, "Here, where I cannot readily make a scene?"

Before either Gilly or Maloney could open their mouths to agree, a scream of pure fury interrupted them.

Gilly was faster than Maloney and he reached the source of the scream before anyone else. It'd come from inside the Krane house, a modern monstrosity that sprawled over the hillside below the vineyards. He rushed through the wide open glass doors, into a room full of chrome and tweed furniture and on into the gallery beyond.

It was Mrs. Krane, fallen backwards atop her hapless son, who'd screamed, and with good reason. There were two sets of thugs fighting over a glass case containing a marble Chinese lion statue, its big paw raised as if it'd been holding something, once. That wasn't the worst of it, however. One—familiar from his appearance in Chinatown's temple—had summoned hundreds of centipedes.

The other group was familiar as well. Gilly had been working as a police officer long enough to run into the different gangs infesting Low Town. Some worked for Crogan, some for Barton and some were imported from a small town north of Strikersport called Bear Gulch. The last were an unusual bunch, well educated and given to wearing much nattier clothing than most of their ilk. They talked pretty, too, a rarity among thugs.

Better class of thug though they might be, this bunch weren't much braver and certainly not any more loyal. Not when faced with a man who could summon insects whose bite left their victims twitching on the floor, foaming at the mouth.

When Gilly skidded into the room, his sudden appearance proved the final straw. The thugs ran for the far door, leaving Gilly faced with the sorcerer. "Well now, this is an interesting turn of events. Imagine meeting you here."

"Get out of my way."

"I don't think so," Gilly said, hearing Mrs. McLeod walk in behind him. "Those thugs were obviously here to steal something, but somehow I have a feeling you are too."

"Wugong," Mrs. McLeod said. "Why am I not surprised you're involved in this folly?"

The man peered at Mrs. McLeod in a confused sort of way. "You. You're that foolish woman of McLeod's. The one who keeps pretending she's Chinese."

"I am American," Mrs. McLeod sighed. "And a daughter of the Jeen Loon. And you are still an idiot, I see."

"You're a poser, pretending—"

Gilly coughed. "It seems you know each other," he said, stepping forward. Drawing on his fires was risky, but he could tell those centipedes were deadly and he knew what would happen if some damned fool injured Meng Huang Hsiang's priestess. "Any other day, I'd leave you two to your reunion. But not here and not now."

The Chinese man turned a nearsighted glare on Gilly. "Stay out of this, *gweilo!*"

Gilly glanced briefly at his tanned hands and cocked his head at Mrs. McLeod. "That means ghost in Chinese, right? Did I suddenly turn into a Caucasian?" His human appearance remained the one he'd taken when the first peoples in this land had drawn him into existence; brown-skinned and black-haired and a bit young to be taken seriously by most men. Until, at least, he set them afire.

"No. Feng Wugong has always had a way of making assumptions about his enemies. Unfortunately, once he does, it is quite difficult to change his mind." Mrs. McLeod drew a fan from her sleeve, batting away the dozen or so centipedes attacking her. "Officer Maloney, assist me in getting the Kranes to safety. Officer Kenneth, you are safer from his toys than most, but their poison is powerful enough to injure the White Serpent. You aren't a God yet. Be careful."

Before Gilly could retort that he wasn't looking to be a God anyway, Mrs. McLeod and Maloney grabbed the Kranes and left him to face Wugong alone.

Gilly and Wugong stared at each other for several long moments before Wugong said grimly, "You don't really think you stand a chance against my insects, do you?"

To be completely honest, Gilly wasn't sure. Oh, if he released his flames, he'd probably char the little bastards to ash. But his mortal flesh made it difficult to control his fire and he didn't want to risk burning down Rosamund's home just to fight off a thief.

Noticing some of Wugong's centipedes scurrying towards him, Gilly slammed a heel down and added as much heat as he dared to the blow. It did the job, to Wugong's obvious surprise. "They don't seem all that tough," Gilly said, shrugging.

"How did you—what did you—"

"I don't think I'm going to answer that." Gilly moved slowly towards his opponent. He'd gotten barely three steps when something flickered in the air off to one side and a woman appeared, clutching a bronze vase from the case against the wall. "Oh yes. I forgot about you."

"Enough playing around, Wugong. I have what we came for. Let's go."

Wugong hesitated, then turned and set off at a run, the woman close behind.

If it weren't for the cry following Wugong's escape, Gilly probably would have let the pair go. Granted, he and Maloney had been sent to provide security for the wine tasting party but no one had asked them to protect it from sorcerers. Wugong wasn't worth his time, not for an antique bronze vase, no matter how expensive.

Except Gilly knew that voice from way back. Rosamund might be more even-tempered than she'd once been, but she still had the vocal talents of a stevedore down on the docks. More importantly, her shout wasn't just anger but actual despair and it hit Gilly straight where he lived.

Rushing after the escapees, he found Rosamund crouching beside her dog. The animal shuddered, clearly in pain, foaming at the mouth and twitching. "Boopsie. No. Please. Tell me you're all right, Boopsie!"

Gilly dropped to his knees beside the dog, knowing there wasn't much chance of saving him from the sorcerer's poison. Except Rosamund grabbed him by the hand, saying, "Help him. Please. You have to help him! I think he's dying!"

This wasn't the first time Gilly had found himself faced with someone begging for his help. It wasn't the first time he'd found himself finding hidden and unexpected depths to his nature. Nor was this the first time he'd found himself wanting desperately to fulfill the thing asked of him, no matter how hard it was to achieve.

Except, even changed as he was, even with the connection his spirit had to the fires of the earth and the shadows of the rift, he simply didn't have the power to heal. It wasn't part of his nature and he found himself pleading in turn; voiceless, wordless, pleas to whatever power might hear him to show him what to do.

Impossibly, because whatever he was, he was no human whose faith could beg miracles, Gilly felt something touch his mind. He lifted his head and squeezed his eyes shut, then opened them again as he realized he wasn't imagining what he saw. The figure was familiar, a full size version of one of the idols from the Jeen Loon. Not Meng Huang Hsiang, either, but the strangest of the eight, the one that combined aspects of both man and woman in its appearance.

No words were said, but none needed to be. The figure's mind touched Gilly's, showing him how to draw on and combine his nature; smoke and fire, ice and void. All into one agonizingly painful tool that drew on his own life to heal another.

Without hesitation, forcing himself not to scream, Gilly turned the gift onto Boopsie, seeking out the poison, simultaneously burning it out of the animal's system and cooling the fever his fire inflicted. The dog whimpered and whined, then slowly sat up, blinking his big dark eyes as he licked Gilly's cheek. Rosamund flung her arms around him, kissing the other cheek.

"Yah!" Gilly grumbled. "Don't do that. You know I don't like it when you do that." At the same time he scrubbed his fingers through the animal's fur and patted Rosamund's shoulder helplessly. He shuddered, fighting down nausea. He needed a rest and he didn't have time.

"Officer Kenneth? Are you all right?"

"No," Gilly told Rosamund. "But I'm going to have to be. You take care of things here. I'll be back."

"Where are you going?"

"You don't think I'm going to let the guy who did this to Boopsie get away without a good solid kick to the backside, do you?" Gilly asked, standing up and swaying a little as he regained his equilibrium.

Rosamund thought about it and suddenly grinned, the expression taking Gilly's breath away, it was so familiar. "No. I don't. Give him hell for me."

"There's my good girl," Gilly said as he set off at a run out the front door. Those two couldn't have gotten far, carrying a great big bronze vase like that.

Running through the vineyard behind the Krane's winery, Gilly felt both the strongest and the weakest he'd ever been. The energy coursing through him wasn't entirely his own. Gifted to him by that strange Khaitanese deity, it was only because they shared similar traits that they'd been able to connect. He wasn't sure he could retain what the Twins had given him, but he'd worry about it later.

The question of dealing with Wugong remained. The old Gilly, the one from before he'd met Rosamund's Aunt Gwendolyn, would have killed more readily. Those days were long over, however. If he had time, or inclination, he'd have studied the idea more carefully, but right that moment he needed to focus on finding and stopping Wugong from escaping. He could care less about the vase, but Wugong had tried to hurt someone he liked and that was never something he approved of.

The thief wasn't far ahead. Gilly could hear him running through the trees and up the mountainside. Wugong knew he was being followed. His centipedes kept appearing, trying to launch themselves into Gilly's face and hair. He charred them without hesitation as he ran, straight into a rocky clearing.

By this time the sound of Wugong's pounding feet had faded and no more centipedes appeared. Gilly skidded to a halt among the jagged rocks and felt a sharp surge of danger. Instinct flung him backwards, but not before hundreds of centipedes boiled up from the ground. Wugong and his partner appeared then, sure of their triumph.

The bites were agony and Gilly felt sudden sympathy for Boopsie and the others the centipedes had bitten. He felt more than a little like falling down and twitching himself. Only fear that death would be a final end to his existence, with no hope of an afterlife, kept him from giving in.

If they'd been back at the house what happened next would have killed everyone nearby. Even here among the rocks wasn't the best place for it, dry as the weather had been lately. Under most circumstances he could control the heat of his inner Self. Injured, exhausted and unabashedly afraid, his blood burned and boiled within him. The centipedes exploded, sparks flying and landing around him.

Knowing what would happen if those sparks fell in among the trees, Gilly flung himself forward, grasping blindly for his enemies. His fingers caught hold of something metal and he felt it melting beneath the heat of his fires. Immediately he steadied, gaining an equilibrium he had never had before when using his fire. The rift inside him would never heal, but it was becoming easier to control, his servant, his partner, instead of feared enemy.

Something moved near him and he heard someone shouting angry curses in Cantonese. Since the insults were, for the most part, quite true, he ignored them in favor of recovering his self-control. He opened his eyes and smiled at Wugong, saying softly, "I try to avoid killing these days. So you're safe for the moment." The mountain shuddered beneath them, responding to his power. "But if I were you, I'd start running home to Canton. Because I doubt I'll give you another chance if you hurt someone under my protection again."

Wugong was the fool Mrs. McLeod said he was and would have stayed right where he was. Fortunately, his partner was a wiser woman than he. She grabbed him by the arm, used her illusions to conceal them both, and set off running.

"And don't come back!" Gilly shouted after them, watching the dust scatter and the brush bend where they passed. Then he sat down and put his head between his knees. "Never been sick before," he muttered to himself. "Guess there's always a first time."

It took a while for Maloney and Mudan to catch up with Gilly, by which time he'd straightened enough to see them coming. He wasn't up to much more, however, so he just watched the pair approach him cautiously.

"Well, now," Maloney said, hands on hips and shaking his head sadly as he gazed down at Gilly, "You're a sight for the sorest of eyes, you are. That Jones fellow's going to be mad, when he's taking a look at that suit of yours."

Gilly's borrowed finery was entirely ruined. The fires inside him had charred and burned the black silk suit. The smell was dark and unpleasant, even to Gilly. He managed a wry smile, "Well, it's not as if I need my pay for much. They can dock it if they like."

"That," Mrs. McLeod said quietly, "will depend on whether Mr. Jones remains employed with Mrs. Krane long enough to complain. Based on their discussion before Officer Maloney and I came to look for you, I think he will no longer be with the family by the time we return."

"He finally gave up on them, huh?"

"No. Interestingly enough, it was Mrs. Krane who wished to part ways with the gentleman. Something about his allowing those thugs to enter the art gallery when it ought to have been properly secured for the day."

Maloney agreed. "She pretty much straight up accused him of working with that lot. Not sure she's wrong, for once." He put a hand beneath Gilly's elbow and helped him to his feet. "Now then, lad. T'is high time you got back down off this rock and took yourself a proper rest."

Vertigo, or at least Gilly thought it was vertigo, nearly had him falling on his knees. He forced himself to stand straight, staring out at the horizon so as not to go sprawling. "I have a feeling there's not going to be much rest for me until this nonsense is over," he grumbled. "Who was that fellow, anyway, Mrs. McLeod? And why does he think you're white?"

"Wugong was an old adversary of mine and Conall's from Shanghai. We had other run-ins, later, but he took it into his head that I couldn't possibly be of Chinese descent." Thoughtfully, Mrs. McLeod added, "I believe he is badly in need of glasses. He is certainly incapable of being corrected."

Gilly had noticed that as well, leaving him to wonder how Wugong's partner managed to get him to cooperate so readily. Still, unless they ran across the man again later, he wasn't the first problem. "Tell me something, Mrs. McLeod, am I right in suspecting there's a great deal more to this than just some rival gangs looking to steal priceless artifacts? Especially since I don't think those Eight Immortal statues of yours are actually priceless?"

"Their value is in their history and their workmanship," Mrs. McLeod agreed. "But yes, I think there is a great deal coming together here. The Twins would not have come to your aid if they did not expect you to act on their behalf in return."

Which, Gilly knew, was a price his kind had to pay, unless he wished to go back to being a mindless, thoughtless, monster. Seeing Rosamund waiting at the gate for them, eyes wide and worried, he knew he desired nothing of the sort.

Quite the contrary, in fact.

Chapter Four
Strikersport's Gold River Casino is Known for its Friendly Atmosphere

It was late afternoon when William Jarvis arrived at the Krane Winery and he was actually surprised by the warmth of his Aunt Harriet's welcome. Their relationship had never been close, especially after she'd tried to deprive him of his inheritance. He'd no wish for revenge, but he neither loved, nor even liked, her. Nor, for that matter, was he terribly fond of his cousins; Rosamund and Peter.

Seeing Rosamund helping Gilly back from whatever trouble the former monster had gotten himself into, William's opinion of her raised several notches. She'd been getting a bit less temperamental since her father died. It was almost as if she saw herself as the family's best representative and wanted to prove it to the world.

As for Peter, complaining to any and every person who would listen that he'd known Jones was a thief from the start and that he'd tried to warn his mother not to hire the man— Well there wasn't much to be done about him. He'd been a self-important bully all his life; William doubted he'd ever change.

Realizing his aunt's most important guest, Mrs. Andersen, was speaking to him, William quickly recalled what she'd asked. "I don't think my aunt will open the gallery today. This incident will have to be investigated. I'm sure our Chief of Police is already sending his men, in fact."

The lady harrumphed in a most elegant way. She was a small, older, woman, a little portly around the waist and so like Harriet Krane in attitude William was surprised the two weren't already the best of friends. "All I want is to look for her *fu* dog."

William didn't know what the lady meant, but noticed a waiter, one of Mudan McLeod's employees, flinch at the term. Ignoring the reaction, he told Mrs. Andersen, "I'm sure the opportunity will present itself soon enough."

"And the towel tee vase. Minerva tells me its one of a kind. I was planning on buying it."

Another flinch from the waiter, so slight William was the only one who noticed. Knowing next to nothing about art, he guessed Mrs. Andersen was butchering the names of the items somehow. Much of the Krane's art gallery consisted of Chinese and Japanese artwork, after all.

Rather than pretend to knowledge he didn't possess, William told the lady, "No doubt my Aunt would be a better person to speak to." He noticed Maloney beckoning him towards the back of the garden and added, "If you'll excuse me, I believe I'm needed elsewhere."

Finding Maloney alone behind a big bushy plant, William asked, "What happened? I got here just when the excitement was over."

Instead of answering, Maloney eyed him dourly. "You're looking pretty fine, these days, Jarvis. Enjoying being a bigshot detective and a resort partner instead of riding around the streets with little old me?"

"I'm still a cop," William reminded Maloney. William's friend and business partner, John Striker, handled the resort's day to day affairs, allowing William to keep his job with the force. Nowadays he headed a special department, one in charge of the sort of investigations becoming more and more common in Strikersport. "Like I keep telling you, Maloney, I do miss being on the streets. It's not my fault Michaels felt I'd be more useful elsewhere."

Usually Maloney scoffed, still considering William the wet-behind-the-ears rookie he'd warned not to trip over his own two feet. This time he looked serious. "Yeah, and it's looking like this is going to be one of those jobs."

Given William had just come from a conference with Chief Michaels on the subject, he wasn't surprised. "I'm guessing this business is more of the same? Officer Kenneth looked like he was dragged headfirst through an ash-heap."

Gilly tended to keep his powers to himself most of the time, and not just because it tired him out. Gilly would deny it entirely, but William had long since realized the former monster didn't like calling on his fire against purely mundane opponents. William suspected Gilly considered his powers an unfair advantage. If he'd had to set himself on fire, there'd been something supernatural involved.

"You're not wrong about there being more," Maloney agreed. "Michaels tell you about them two Chinee—Chinese, sorry—who showed up 'round about the end of the fight in the temple? The ones that shadow snakey thing scared off?"

"He did."

"They were here just now. Them two and a gang I'm pretty near sure come from Bear Gulch. They're the only toughs I know who get their selves all gussied up like they were going to th' opera."

Bear Gulch's crime rate had skyrocketed recently, in part due to the new boss, a man named Horne. Before Crogan went straight, or at least pretended to, he and Horne had been at frequent odds. If he were involved, there were at least three separate groups poking around in Strikersport's business. "You think Horne's trying to take over Crogan's old territory, now he's legit?"

Maloney snorted at the thought of Crogan being legit in any way, shape, or form. "Might be, yeah. You could be asking him about it. I think he's here for the party."

William made a note to himself to do that very thing. For the moment, though, there was still the question of Gilly's condition. "You haven't told me what happened to Officer Kenneth?"

"That Chinese fellow from the temple—Wiggins or something like— did some nasty magic work. Waved his hands and threw a whole nest of centipedes at Kenneth. Our boy did his usual thing, but from what Mrs. McLeod says, them centipedes can do a number even on supernatural types. He's going to be all right, but it might be a bit before he's walking around easy like."

William considered that. "I'm glad he kept that fellow from hurting anyone. Was anything stolen?"

"Don't know about Boss Horne's men, but that Wiggins fellow ran off with some sort of, what was it Mrs. McLeod called it? Tah ou tee ay vase. 'Cept Kenneth got a bit hot under the collar, fighting off them centipedes and melted it."

Tah ou tee ay wasn't a term William recognized but he remembered Mrs. Andersen's desire to buy something with a similar name. Towel Tee, she'd called it. Could it be the same item? That was another thing he'd have to ask about, once he was done talking to Crogan. "Right. You go back to keeping an eye on things. I'd best get to work, myself."

Maloney agreed, leaving William to his own devices.

William found Crogan sampling wine at the back of the garden, a thoughtful expression on his face as he sipped each glass, spit out the excess and rinsed his mouth. William, who'd watched his grandfather do much the same, was only surprised Crogan knew what he was doing. "They still haven't overcome that sweetness," Crogan said when he noticed William. "It's fine for red wines, but this is a sauvignon blanc. It's supposed to be dryer."

"Just so you know, I don't drink," William pointed out. "So I have no idea what you mean."

"A Krane who doesn't drink. Just doesn't seem right." Crogan toasted William with his latest glass, then set it down. "And whatever it is I'm supposed to have done, I didn't do it."

William doubted Crogan's innocence but they both knew that. "I actually wanted to discuss Horne's doings in Strikersport. Got a moment?"

Crogan frowned furiously. "Is that rat bastard trying again?"

"Let's talk about it and see?" William led Crogan to a quiet corner. "Did you hear about a fight over in Chinatown?" He'd be surprised if Crogan hadn't. After all, a man in his position had to have some idea of any criminal doings going on in town.

"I heard there was a bit of a dustup," Crogan admitted. "Like I said, I didn't have a thing to do with it. I don't stick my fingers in Chinatown anymore. Cheh would have my gonads for *dim sum* if I did."

Unsurprised the 'former' gangster was on a first name basis with the boss of Chinatown, William said, "It's got all the earmarks of the kind of business I'm supposed to keep an eye out for."

"Oh dear God. Not again."

"Gods, apparently. Four of them. Maybe eight, if we're unlucky." William could see from Crogan's reaction he'd no idea what had happened. Of course, Crogan didn't like involving himself in the sort of messes William was supposed to be keeping an eye on, so he was probably on the level. This time.

"That Meng Huang Hsiang—ow!" Crogan slapped the back of his neck as if bitten, adding, "I'll learn not to say his name someday. It always gets attention."

Quite likely it did, but they weren't there to discuss the Mad God. Or, rather, they weren't there to discuss him specifically. "Is there any chance Horne would dabble in that sort of thing? Maloney thinks his lot were involved in the robbery here."

"I doubt he knows it exists. Though if he's sending his men this way, he's

" IT IS A REPLICA FROM BATSU VILLAGE ... "

going to find out pretty damned fast." Crogan shrugged. "I've heard he's in town. He's negotiating the sale of some property in Bear Gulch with a fellow named Andersen. I understand they're meeting at my casino."

William was surprised. "You're permitting this?"

"As long as Horne doesn't stick his nose in my business, I don't care. It's money in my bank vault and it all spends the same." Crogan shrugged off William's expression with a bland one of his own. "If he's willing to risk having his plans overheard by making them right in the middle of my territory, who am I to argue?"

William considered the idea. "Mr. Andersen is a guest at the Jewel Island Resort. Striker was going to be meeting him at your casino, but now I think I might take his place. Any objections?"

"Why would I care? After all, the resort brings in guests. Its junior partner is always welcome at Gold River Casino. Just try not to get involved in anything shady, please. I do have a legitimate business to run, after all."

"It is called a *tao tie* mask," Mrs. McLeod told William when he found her to ask about the vase Gilly had destroyed. "The name means gluttonous ogre in English, a design found on *Shang* dynasty bronzeware. What it represents, however, is not known."

William vaguely remembered that the *Shang* dynasty ruled several thousand years ago. He blanched, asking, "Then the vase was expensive?"

"I am more than slightly sure it was a reproduction. One sold to your Aunt for five hundred dollars from the Jeen Loon. I will have to check our records, but I believe we bought it a year or so after the War."

"Can you prove how much it cost, if my aunt tries to get Chief Michaels to recompense her for the damage?"

"I can. But she seems oddly resigned to its loss. I'm not entirely sure why, given her fondness for acquiring money from those around her." Mrs. McLeod slid a platter of meatballs onto a tray and sent it out with a girl just barely big enough to handle the thing. "I may be mistaken, but I almost think she is relieved."

Surprised, because Mrs. McLeod was all too right about Aunt Harriet's tendencies, William tried to think why she'd feel that way. Then he remembered what Mrs. Andersen had said earlier. "Do you know if Mrs. Andersen wanted to buy it? She was talking about a towel tee, but—"

"Oh, she did," Rosamund said suddenly from behind William. She leaned around him to pick up a bottle of whiskey from the sideboard beside Mrs. McLeod. "Mummy was quite put out. I think she's afraid to sell anything she can't prove is the real thing after what happened with Aunt Gwennie's house."

Muttering under his breath, "That never stopped her before," William added, "Why was she put out, and should you be drinking that?"

"You silly man, this is for Gilly, not for me. The poor boy is malingering." Rosamund considered William's other question for a moment and finally said, "Mummy doesn't like Mrs. Andersen. Says she's too pushy. Besides, Mrs. Andersen was sure the thing's thousands of years old."

"Which it was not, if it was the vase my father sold Mrs. Krane. It is a replica from Batsu Village, in Western China," Mudan stated, handing Rosamund a plate of little sandwiches. "Oddly enough, so is the *shi shi* statue Mrs. Andersen wishes to buy."

"That's right. Mummy was afraid of what'd happen when Mrs. Andersen's appraiser realized."

William could see the sense in that. Much of his Aunt's behavior involved keeping up appearances of a wealth and significance he'd long since realized was a veneer of the thinnest gold possible. "It would be a bit of a fuss, wouldn't it?"

"Exactly," Rosamund confirmed, eyes bright as she contemplated the results of such a revelation and proving she still had a touch of a mean streak, no matter how much she'd grown.

Choosing not to say as much, William indicated the bottle, glass, and plate his cousin was gathering. "Did you say Gilly is malingering? Surely not."

"He can be such a lazy bum, sometimes, can't he? But he was badly hurt and he did help Boopsie here. So I can hardly leave him to suffer, now can I?" Rosamund smirked, glancing coquettishly through a doorway off to the side of the kitchen.

Looking through, William saw Gilly sitting behind the former butler's desk, looking frail and terribly pathetic. If he didn't know the man only too well, he would have had more sympathy. As it was, William suspected Gilly was getting all the attention he needed or wanted from the one he needed and wanted it from most.

"You run along and take care of him, then. And tell him I'm coming to talk later."

Once Rosamund had gone on, stealing a plate of little sandwiches as well as everything else, William returned his attention to Mrs. McLeod.

"What is a *tao tie*, anyway? Is it something dangerous and are we looking at a similar situation as when The Voice kept trying to steal that statue of yours?"

"As I've said, in most of China the *tao tie* is a mysterious and unknown thing. A design placed upon old vessels that may or may not have had meaning. In Khaitan—"

Khaitan was that mysterious and magical country Meng Huang Hsiang was supposed to come from and William braced himself. "Is it one of those Immortals of yours?"

"No." Before William could sigh with relief, Mrs. McLeod added, "It is the mount for the Twins, the Immortal in charge of the Northeastern province of Khaitan."

William remembered the statues in the Jeen Loon, "The Twins. The one you can't tell if it's a boy or a girl? The one with four arms?"

"Yes. The twins are male in winter, female in summer. In spring and fall, they begin to shift from one to the other. They are the weakest and gentlest of the Immortals but even they are not ones to cross."

"You said the *tao tie* is their mount? Like your God's tiger?"

Mrs. McLeod inclined her head. "Indeed. Its appearance changes, depending on who you are and how you look upon it. Treat it politely, should you run across it."

Worriedly, William asked, "Am I likely to?"

"If the Twins were freed, their mount is free as well. I think it possible. Though I believe they have found one to work through already." Mrs. McLeod gave a significant look back at Gilly, who was basking in Rosamund's attention and ignoring everything outside the office. "He is a study in contrasts, just as the Twins are. He gives them the connection to this world they need, their flesh and blood form being in Khaitan."

William just hoped all those Gods, minor and weak though they were away from home, didn't decide to bring on Ragnarok, or Armageddon or whatever End of the World scenario was appropriate for Khaitanese deities.

"Honestly, I have no idea why that Wugong fellow wanted the vase. Or the other thugs, for that matter." Gilly sipped the whiskey Rosamund had poured him and sighed peacefully. "There is one thing. I have a feeling Mummy is right about Jones being involved."

Though he raised a brow at Gilly referring to Aunt Harriet as mummy, William spread his hands, asking, "Why?"

"Rosamund just told me the gallery was locked up tighter than a drum earlier this morning. Something about not wanting to let certain people like Crogan in. Not that I blame her in the slightest. There's still a few spots of rust on that man's armor." Gilly grinned at a mental image William chose not to contemplate, adding, "In which case, how the devil did those thieves get in? Not to mention Wugong and his partner. Granted, the one seems to have some sort of illusion magic, but she and that idiot Wugong were busy in Chinatown a good part of the morning."

"Idiot?"

"Idiot," Gilly confirmed. "Mrs. McLeod could tell you more about him, if you really want to know. But he's the sort that gets an idea in his head and won't ever let go even when faced with the exact opposite facts."

Considering that a common problem, William didn't bother addressing it. "Mrs. McLeod said something about the Twins making use of you."

"They, he, she, whatever they are, probably are." Gilly sounded calm, but he looked troubled at the thought. "I'd bet all four of the younger set are looking for human, or not quite human, focal points. Or were."

"Were?"

"Don't quote me on this, but Monkey and the Serpent have already found someone. I wasn't there when Miss Frazier and Dragon rescued Mrs. Andersen and her friend, but I felt some old power. And I saw the Serpent's shadows talking to that kid from the newspaper. Lee, I think his name is."

Remembering what Mrs. McLeod had said about the Twins finding Gilly compatible somehow, William asked, "Any guess as to why?"

"This is the sort of thing you should be asking Mrs. McLeod, you know. I'm no expert on Khaitanese Gods," Gilly pointed out. "Though I admit, I've heard things, over the years. Monkey's a trickster. It'd be like him to choose someone completely out of their depth and see how well they swim. If so, Miss Frazier managed with flying colors. As for the Serpent, he approves of calm and collected forethought and Lee has that in spades. Did you see how he handled driving through the hailstorm last month? Impeccable."

William made a note to check in with both Miss Frazier and Lee when he had the chance. "Who's the last of the four?"

"Fellow called the Black Eagle, I believe. I think he is, or was, some sort of outlaw. Never did get a good idea of why he was one of the Eight. Of course, the only one I've ever dealt with before now was—the Mad One—so I can't be sure."

"Any thoughts on which way he'd go, looking for someone to work through?"

"At a guess? I'd say he'd be looking at criminals. The docks maybe?" Gilly shrugged. "I'm not really sure and I have a feeling I'm not supposed to know. All I can say is, somewhere where crime, or at least sin, is common?"

William could think of one place such things could be found, in abundance. "Like the casino?"

"Why yes," Gilly agreed, grinning broadly. "That sounds just the place. When we going, boss?"

It was mid-afternoon by the time they reached Gold River Casino and William wasn't entirely sure why he'd allowed not only Gilly to come along for the ride, but Rosamund as well. Not to mention Boopsie, because where the mistress went, the faithful wolfhound followed.

Gilly, at least, made sense. He knew about magic and the supernatural; hell, he was supernatural. But Rosamund's only real talent was screaming the house down, or so it seemed to William. She'd been pleasantly quiet for the trip down Krane Peak, across the river and back up to the casino overlooking the valley between the two mountains. The land had belonged to Mr. Chang and was under lease as part of Chang and Crogan's business agreement.

A handsomely dressed valet took William's car, while another greeted him and his companions without batting an eye. Gilly was back in uniform, with Rosamund looking appropriately dressed in the outfit she'd worn for the garden party. She clung to Gilly's arm in a way that made the former monster look both embarrassed and a little smug.

"Would sir care for a private room to dine?"

"I'm actually hoping to speak with Mr. Andersen. I understand he's here?"

"I believe he is in the Pacifica Hall, sir. However, if I may suggest—" The man looked William and Gilly up and down significantly. "Perhaps a change of clothes is in order? Mr. Crogan keeps a variety of evening dress for those of his guests who lack the appropriate attire."

Gilly sighed. "You mean we gotta get all monkey-suited again?"

"I'm afraid so, Officer Kenneth. The common areas are open to any-one, but there is a dress code we ask guests to adhere to when visiting the Pacifica Hall."

"We may as well." William decided, to Rosamund's clear pleasure. She liked playing dress-up.

Gilly raised a brow. "Do you really want me and Rosie here to come with you?"

"You know what I want you to be doing," William told him, "As well as keeping Rosamund out of trouble."

Rosamund giggled. "What about Gilly, though. Who's going to keep an eye on him?"

"Naturally, you are, cousin." Not that William really expected either to be very good at the job. But he wanted them where he could keep an eye on them, especially with ancient Khaitanese Gods wandering the landscape. For all he knew, that Black Eagle fellow would attach himself to Gilly as well. No one had said it was impossible, after all.

The inside of Pacifica Hall was a fantasia of oceanic life. The walls were painted in blue and green, with fronds of seaweed carved into the plaster. Seahorses and otters frolicked in the waves and pretty metal fish hung from strands high above them. A giant octopus hung from the ceiling, holding eight aqua-tinted bulbs.

William eyed the octopus and wondered if Crogan knew about the one who lived beneath Jewel Island. Herself was another of Strikersport's inhuman and supernatural inhabitants, a sentient being who would—for the price of a meal—answer a single question. According to Gilly, she was a God, but not for the humans who came to beg her aid. Apparently there was a colony of intelligent octopi? octopods? living off to the west of Strikersport, deep beneath the ocean.

Shaking off his curiosity, William searched the room for Mr. Andersen. They'd never met, but Gilly knew the man by face and pointed him out readily. "I'm not sure he'll recognize me, but he might. It was a bit chaotic in the temple."

The man in question was sitting alone in an alcove near the bar, his ex-pression dour as he checked his watch. "Let me do the talking," William ordered and was a little surprised when both Gilly and Rosamund folded their hands innocently. No one who knew either would believe it, but William had the oddest feeling they really meant to behave.

Reflecting either Gilly was good for Rosamund or Rosamund was good for Gilly, William approached quietly. "Mr. Andersen?"

"And who might you be?" Andersen demanded, sounding like he might have had a bit too much to drink. "Another local with a proposition for making a load of money off me? A journalist? I talked to that Lee boy earlier."

William managed not to let his irritation show. Money was one thing he didn't want more of. Smiling in as friendly a manner as he could muster, he said, "I'll leave the propositions to my partner, Mr. Striker. He handles our business quite well without my clumsy assistance."

"Oh. You must be the Krane boy. The one who plays cops and robbers in this tiny podunk city while Striker does the work."

Having heard that sort of insult before, William ignored it. "I'm William Jarvis, sir. I inherited my portion of the Krane holdings from my mother." He indicated the booth "May we sit?"

"We?" Andersen repeated and turned his gaze on Rosamund and Gilly. "Who are they when they're at home?"

As politely as he could manage, William explained, "This is my cousin, Rosamund Krane. The gentleman is Gilly Kenneth, an associate of mine." He didn't mention the nature of their association. He also ignored the slight snort Gilly gave at being called a gentleman. "They have some interest in the resort as well."

Andersen's eyes narrowed as he looked Gilly over. "They let bloody Indians in here?"

Stiffening, because it honestly hadn't occurred to him the man would be so rude, William said, "Gilly is a trusted friend and associate. I hardly think his family background has anything to do with that."

"And it isn't your business who they let in here anyway," Rosamund snapped. "His money is just as good as anyone else's."

"I doubt there's much I can do to help you here, William," Gilly added and if his voice was quieter, there was an underlying heat to it William recognized. "Might be better if I went looking for that—friend—of Crogan's. We have business with him, too, remember?"

Reminded Horne was supposed to be meeting Mr. Andersen at the casino, William agreed.

"Yes, Squanto. Do go on—YIPE!" Andersen's insult was interrupted by the sudden flare of heat and smoke from the candle sitting at his table. It didn't—quite—take out the man's mustache, but it was too close for comfort.

William didn't bother looking at Gilly, knowing the flare was the former monster's doing. He wasn't sure he minded, given the provocation. Instead, he sat across from Mr. Andersen and said, "Gilly is one of the richest men in Strikersport, sir. It might not be the wisest idea to offend him."

"Him? Rich?"

"He has access to more gold, silver and other fine metals than anyone else I know," William answered truthfully. Gilly's fires came from the earth and he could draw on its riches when he really needed to. Not that he often did.

Andersen watched the pair leaving the bar area with a dour frown. "Well, whatever. What are you looking for, boy? And, just so you know, my secretary isn't here at the moment. Don't know where the man's run off to, but I do need him for business."

William inclined his head. "That would be Mr. Rogers, right? I was told he'd gone missing this morning. Hopefully the police will find him quickly. In the meantime, perhaps we could discuss the generalities?"

"Such as?"

"Well, among other things, I wanted to ask about your plans for the future with the Jewel Island Resort. John was hoping to find out if you've decided anything about making us your exclusive destination of choice for your executives."

"Ah, yes. I did mention that to Mr. Striker. It's a difficult decision. There are other possibilities, you know. Both in Strikersport and Bear Gulch. Mr. Horne and I have worked together before."

Knowing what was expected of him, William beckoned the barkeep. "Let me buy you a drink and discuss those possibilities. Perhaps we can come to an agreement."

"—thing we do like about the resort is its marina. This casino is quite pleasant, of course, and Mr. Crogan has been an excellent host, but he tends to permit questionable characters in. Why I saw an old man in rags over in the baccarat room just an hour or so ago."

That old man was probably Francis Trendle's father but William didn't bother saying so. After his retirement, George Trendle had stopped worrying about appearances, preferring to dress and act as he wished. "Up here?" he asked.

"Well, no. But—"

"Coming from the background he does, Mr. Crogan is something of an egalitarian. As he says, everyone's money spends the same. Naturally, he does try to segregate the hoi polloi away from among the common folk."

Mr. Andersen frowned, as if almost realizing the implied insult. Then he looked off to the side and raised a hand, calling, "Athena, my dear. You look stunning. Did you enjoy yourself at that garden party?"

Realizing Mrs. Andersen had arrived, William rose to his feet as quickly and smoothly as he could. "Ma'am, a pleasure to see you again."

She frowned at him, "Do I know you? Oh, yes, that nice young man at the garden party." Returning her attention to her husband, she added, "I found a lovely *fu* dog—"

The woman behind her said, in a voice suggesting she'd repeated the words far too many times, "*Shi shi*, Athena."

"Oh yes, that's right. *shi shi*. They really shouldn't call them *fu* dogs when they aren't dogs at all," Mrs. Anderson said disparagingly. "Anyway, I've found a fine statue to bring home with us. That silly woman over at the winery tried to keep me from looking at it, but I insisted. I even got a discount—it's just the male and he's missing his ball—so that should make you happy."

While William tried not to react to the description, Andersen sighed. "If it's the one you and Minerva were talking about, it's too damned big to bring on the plane, Athena."

"Nonsense. We'll just pay for the extra weight. They won't mind."

Guessing the *shi shi* in question was the one from his Aunt Harriet's gallery, William forced himself not comment. It was easily two-hundred pounds and unwieldy to boot. He couldn't think of any commercial airline that would willingly carry the thing. Still, Mrs. Andersen seemed the sort to ignore anything that didn't suit her. It would be better to just let the Andersens work out the problem for themselves.

Unsure what to do, William glanced around the crowded dining room and noticed a commotion towards the middle. Somehow, Mrs. Andersen had brought Aunt Harriet's stone lion all the way from the winery to the casino. That didn't surprise, or even worry him, nearly so much as the more obvious problem. The lion was coming to life and it looked as hungry as any beast might that had sat still for unknown centuries.

William stared for several breathless and terrified moments, paralyzed by the sight. The lion stretched, a slow, leisurely movement that shifted to sudden action as it shook its head and leapt from its plinth. It landed inside the bar, shattering the wooden floor with its weight. Then it stalked forward, stone mane flowing impossibly around his shoulders as it roared.

That broke William's paralysis and he rose to his feet, though he'd no idea what to do. The others in the room were running for the door, their screams drawing the lion's attention. Only Gilly's sudden appearance, blocking the thing's path, kept it from nabbing the nearest escapee with its claws. "Oh, no, you don't," Gilly growled. "Don't make me use my outdoor voice."

"Can you stop it?" William demanded.

"I'd kill everyone here if I tried to melt that marble," Gilly answered grimly. "I can hold him off while people get out, though."

"No one is going anywhere," a voice said from behind the lion. The speaker was hidden beneath a hooded yellow robe, but William thought he caught a glimpse of a young man's face in the shadows. He held something in his hands, a squirming pale object that looked like a smaller version of the adult lion. "I'll have the justice I came for, no matter who must suffer for it."

"Justice?" William repeated. "Attacking strangers who happen to be in the way is justice?"

The man moved forward, the lion cub in his hands mewling unhappily in his grip, causing the adult to growl furiously. "You're not my target, *gweilo*. Neither you, or your pet monster. Better run. You don't have the power to stop my justice. I am the law, come to punish the guilty."

"Justice? Law? What do you mean?"

"Ask the ones behind you in the afterlife, when the Judge of all things calls you to order. Or get out of the way and leave those fools behind you to me." The man moved forward, smiling viciously.

Behind William, Mr. Andersen snapped, "Rogers, what the devil are you playing at? Put that stupid lion down and come here. You have work to do."

"I have work to do, yes. The work of vengeance. The work of justice. The Black Eagle demands you pay for your crimes!" Rogers shook the lion cub, causing the larger one to growl furiously. "You. Do our God's will! Obey me!"

With a frustrated roar, the lion stalked forward, crouching. Gilly was blocking the statue's path, but William knew he couldn't stop the thing. Seeing the lion's reluctant movements and realizing why, William flung himself at Rogers, intending to snatch the baby from its captor.

The floor rose up between them before William reached the man. "Gilly!"

"On it, boss."

The wood smoldered and Rogers screamed, nearly dropping the baby lion as he clutched his head. Hoping Gilly could keep his fire under control, William dodged around the twisted wood, leaping for Rogers again. This time he was fast enough, barreling into the man and knocking him to the floor.

"No! My vengeance! My justice!"

"Forcing a father to kill by threatening his baby isn't justice." William wasn't sure how he knew the cub and the adult lion were related but he didn't doubt it, either. "Vengeance isn't justice!" He and Rogers rolled around on the floor, each struggling to catch hold of the cub.

With a yowl of terror, the animal slipped free of Roger's grip and set off running out the door. Immediately, the lion spun around on his hindquarters, leaping for Rogers now. Realizing it would gladly kill the man, William automatically shouted, "No! Bad lion. No!" Even as he did so, he wondered if he'd gone mad. What was he going to do? Swat the animal with a rolled up newspaper?

The lion growled at him and to William's utter surprise, seemed to cower. Only when a voice spoke in William's ear, a soaring clarion call, did he realize why. Something hovered over him, black wings flapping as it spoke in a language almost like Chinese, yet not quite. Talons tightened gently on William's shoulder as the words shifted and changed inside William's head. He corrected himself. The words weren't shifting, his own comprehension was.

"You'll do. You will do. The law is the law, but it must be tempered. It must be mastered, lest it master you." Before William could ask a single question the voice continued, "Enough, my servant. You need not fight yet. Rest until you're needed. This man is my Speaker. Assist him when the time comes."

The lion whimpered and William knew why. "I'll find your cub and make sure it gets into safe hands, I promise."

The lion gazed intently into William's eyes, then bowed and returned to his plinth, becoming stone again. The sound of wings fluttered around William, a flare of brightness half-blinding him for a moment. When it faded, the presence in William's thoughts was gone as well, leaving behind something he couldn't quite put name to.

Slowly understanding what must have happened, William said softly, "Black Eagle, I presume?"

"And that," Gilly said, equally quietly, "makes four."

Chapter Five
Trendle Tower has Many Opportunities for Entertainment

Screams and shouts warned Robby before he spotted the crowd running down the stairs. Well practiced at evasion, he stepped to the side, avoiding the oncoming rush just barely in time. Dozens of well-dressed, normally self-possessed, men and women stampeded past, too panicked to notice him or Crogan's guards. The poor men were being trampled in the rush.

Twisting and shifting to get past the herd, Robby whistled cheerfully as he moved. There was trouble ahead and he was curious to see what. He could have called for help, of course, but then he'd owe the nuisance again. Better to wait and see what was going on first.

Noticing a vaguely familiar figure pushing her way past the crowd a dozen or so feet ahead of him, Robby hurried forward. Miss Frazier was a nice, brave, young woman but she was small and relatively slight. Admittedly, so was Robby's mother, but Miss Frazier didn't know how to fight. He didn't want to see her hurt for her courage.

At last the stampede trickled to nothing, giving Robby free space to continue. By this time he'd lost track of Miss Frazier and he climbed three steps at a time, only to nearly trip over something round and bulky. Looking down, he realized it was a stone lion cub, its body quivering with terror. He scooped it up gently, tucking it into his zipped up jacket. "Now, now," he said. "You're all right. Just let me check on Miss Frazier, then I'll take you to my ma. She'll know what to do."

The sound of shouting drew Robby's attention and he continued up the steps, reaching the top just as Miss Frazier, in an attack that would have done Robby's Uncle Tan proud, smacked a robed figure in the belly with a six-foot staff. Her victim stumbled backwards, running into Robby and knocking them both down to the landing below.

On his feet instantly, Robby recognized the stranger immediately. This was the man who'd dropped him and Simon down the hatch back at the temple. Though dressed like a Buddhist priest—of sorts—he wore a suit beneath the saffron robe, along with an oddly familiar topaz brooch. Aunt Hikaru had mentioned it, the last time she was in America, hadn't she? Something about possession and vengeful ghosts?

The man flailed, trying to get past and Robby protested, "Hey! Be careful." Inside his jacket, the cub whimpered and he patted it comfortingly. "There's no need to be rude."

"Filthy half-breed, don't get in the way of my justice!" the man snapped, speaking perfect Khaitanese. The floor twisted between them, reshaping itself into an almost humanoid form.

Instinct took over and Robby drew his chain-whip, flicking on its energy field. Guessing quickly, he aimed it at the brooch, breaking it in half. For a moment he wasn't sure if he was right, but then the man collapsed, his wooden creation crashing to the ground a moment later.

Robby picked up the brooch's remains, saying, "Now don't be that way. You're the one ran into me. You should be more careful. Someone could get hurt."

Right then Miss Frazier came into view, her eyes wide and a little scared. She still carried a mahogany staff with gold fittings and Robby forced himself not to react to the sight. "Oh, hello there, Miss Frazier. Do you know what's going on? Everyone was running scared and this man just ran right into me. It's all very confusing."

"That's Mr. Rogers," Miss Frazier said, sounding more than a little frazzled. "What happened to him? Did you—"

"Like I said, he ran into me just now. Quite literally. He tried to hit me and I had to defend myself. I did try not to injure him, but really, there's only so much I could do. I'm afraid I might have been a bit rough." Robby eyed Miss Frazier curiously. "Are you hurt? I've never seen you carry a stick before. He didn't attack you, did he? If he did—"

"Don't worry about it, Mr. McLeod—"

Robby interrupted quickly. "Please. Robby. Mr. McLeod's my father and even he doesn't like being called that, even though Grandfather McLeod died two years ago and—"

"Robby then. I'm not hurt, I promise you."

Grinning a little to himself, because he knew she'd interrupted just to stop him from talking, Robby said, "I'm glad to hear it. Where did you get

" THE THING SLOWLY SHRANK DOWN ... "

that staff anyway? It looks familiar and—"

The next interruption came from the two men hurrying up behind Miss Frazier; William Jarvis and Gilly Kenneth. The former looked frazzled, an expression he often got in situations like this. At the sight of the lion cub peeking out from Robby's jacket, however, relief flooded his face, telling Robby the man knew about the little one and had been worried.

Fortunately for Robby's peace of mind, the officer simply asked, "Miss Frazier, Robby. What happened? Are you two all right?"

Miss Frazier got in ahead of Robby. "I'm fine. I'm not sure why, but Mr. Rogers just attacked me."

The way Miss Frazier spoke made Robby suspect there was more to it than that. Blithely, he added, "I think he might have been possessed by something, or controlled. I'm not sure which. He was speaking Khaitanese. Admittedly that doesn't mean much; my father speaks the language quite well. But he was using the exact same magic as the priest in the temple and it's hard to believe there are two sorcerers around animating the inanimate."

Mr. Jarvis opened his mouth, but Miss Frazier spoke first. "Magic? Sorcerer? Mr. McLeod—Robby, are you out of your—" Her expression shifted as Robby looked significantly at the staff in her hand. He wasn't sure why Sun Wukong had loaned her his weapon but she surely knew it wasn't normal. "What is going on here?" she continued helplessly.

Gilly examined the staff, then grinned broadly at Mr. Jarvis and Robby. "I had a feeling Miss Frazier was going to be involved," he said. "This belongs to that Monkey God, all right."

"I thought so," Robby agreed. "I'm not sure why he'd loan it to Miss Frazier. I don't think she's been trained to fight. Or have you, Miss Frazier? I don't like to make assumptions about things like that. There's no reason you couldn't. My mother taught me and Chou after all and it's a good idea to know a little about self-defense. You never know—"

Gilly turned a disbelieving look on him. "Do you always have to run at the mouth, kid?"

"No," Robby said and couldn't help grinning, "I just like to."

"Gilly, don't pick fights. This isn't the time." Mr. Jarvis turned his attention on Miss Frazier, "You're Mr. Rose's assistant. The one he makes do all the work, right?"

"I'm one of your employees," Miss Frazier agreed. "And Mr. Rose is my immediate superior."

An amused expression crossed Mr. Jarvis' face. "A tactful way to avoid admitting he's a lazy slob who'd rather sit in his office filling out crosswords and leave the work to you," he told her. Which, when Robby thought about it, was pretty much true. He'd called the fellow earlier to let him know the cost of repairing the bus and had been told to talk to Miss Frazier because the whole business was her responsibility.

Miss Frazier stammered, "I—I really couldn't say." At a guess, Robby thought she shared Mr. Jarvis' opinion and that she was relieved, even a bit pleased, to know her boss' boss knew what a useless lump Rose was. "Do you want me to do anything?"

"Well, for one, you might put that staff away before someone notices it. I'd rather we didn't draw too much attention." Mr. Jarvis paused and glanced at the man Robby had knocked out. "And we're going to have to do something about him. Gilly?"

"On it, boss."

As Gilly slung the skinny red-head over his shoulder, Robby told Miss Frazier helpfully, "The staff shrinks, or should. Its owner just thinks of the size and shape he needs." He indicated her hair, fallen around her face in curly, rebellious, strands. "I'd suggest maybe a hairpin? That's nice and unnoticeable and you do seem to have lost a few already."

"That's enough, Robby," Mr. Jarvis said, though he grinned to take the edge off the order. "I think she gets the point. Miss Frazier, could you try what Robby suggested? It would make things easier."

Miss Frazier held the staff in front of her, glaring at it until the thing slowly shrank down and bent in half. It still looked like lacquered wood with gold fittings, but it was small and dark enough to be barely visible against her hair.

Mr. Jarvis eyed her thoughtfully, saying to Gilly, "So you're right about the Monkey King choosing her."

"You mean a little boy named Wukong?" Miss Frazier asked suddenly. "That's what Chou called him, this morning. He's the one who gave me the thing."

Mr. Jarvis looked confused. "Wugong? Wait, that's the fellow with the centipedes, right?"

"No," Robby said quickly. "The names sound similar, but they're written differently in both Chinese and Khaitanese. The man with the centipedes is an old family enemy. Feng Wugong. He's a sorcerer from Canton who ran afoul of my parents in Shanghai—and elsewhere. Monkey's full name is Sun Wukong. Completely different. Better stick with Monkey, though, just to avoid confusion. Though he'd probably prefer Great Sage, Second to None. He usually does. And he's not really a little boy."

Sounding confused and worried, Miss Frazier said. "I don't understand this. I don't understand any of this. What is going on here, Mr. Jarvis?"

"Call me William. Both of you. It looks like we've been dumped into an interesting situation," William said. "We'll have to explain as we go. Come along back to the Pacifica Hall. I want to make sure the Andersens are alright first."

Since he could already guess he was going to be needed, Robby didn't hesitate to agree.

Robby had never been in the casino's Pacifica Hall before and he allowed himself a moment to wander around examining the decorations. Behind him, he could hear Mr. Andersen remonstrating the still unconscious Mr. Rogers for his disappearance earlier in the day. This despite William's attempt to point out that the man was in no fit state for talking.

"I'm telling you, Rogers, this is coming out of your paycheck. And what is that damned outfit you're in? It looks like something those Batsu people would wear!"

"I don't think he cares at the moment, sir," William tried to say. At the same time Robby frowned, a little surprised. Mr. Andersen was right about those robes Mr. Rogers wore, but how did he know anything about Batsu Village?

"He'll care when I'm done with him," Mr. Andersen snapped, unaware of Robby's scrutiny.

"No doubt. But at the moment he can't even hear you. Shouldn't you worry about your wife? She doesn't look at all well."

The lady in question was leaning against her companion, a woman who looked so much like Mrs. Andersen the only way to tell the two apart was by the more elaborate and costly clothes the one wore. Well, that and Robby doubted Mrs. Andersen would be nearly as solicitous. Chou had waxed eloquent on the subject earlier that day and anyone who could throw a fit over a statue, whatever they called it and wherever it'd come from, wasn't the sort to care about others.

Wandering over to the lion statue sitting in the middle of the room, Robby put a hand on its shoulder. It was cold stone now, but it must have been terrifying when it'd moved. He'd have to ask his mother if she had any thoughts on how to combat this sort of magic. Hopefully soon. He had a feeling this wasn't over. Absent-mindedly, he petted the cub in his jacket. "Don't worry about your daddy," he told it. "We'll take good care of him, too."

"If it weren't for what that man tried to do to me, I wouldn't believe it came to life," Miss Frazier said, walking up to join Robby. William and Gilly were still busy with Mr. Andersen, while Rosamund Krane sat with the wife, trying to talk her into waking up, leaving Stephanie without anything to do but fret. "Is this really happening?"

Robby looked down at her and smiled reassuringly, he hoped. "I'd say go back to work and leave it to those who know how to handle it," he told her. "But you're already involved. Even if you did go, you'd still wind up dragged into this. Better to know what's happening. Mother says, 'ignorance is bliss, but it doesn't make the water in the pot stop boiling'."

"My mother says something like that, too," Miss Frazier told him as the marble cub stuck its head out from Robby's jacket. "My God! Another?"

"I found it on the stairway," Robby admitted. "I'll take it to my mother when we have time. She'll know what to do."

The cub made a little meeping sound and Miss Frazier put a cautious finger on its forehead. "It looks just like that ceramic statue your brother sold Mrs. Andersen," she said softly. "So cute."

While Robby agreed, skritching the cub's chin, Miss Frazier continued, "But how can it, and this big one move? You said magic? Sorcerers? I don't understand any of this."

Robby smiled. "Most people don't realize magic exists," he told her. "Just as well, too. It can cause more trouble than it's worth sometimes. Especially if you don't know what you're doing or if you let it rule you."

"Maybe it's better left alone?"

"Easier said than done. Once you realize magic exists and learn to connect with it, it isn't a thing you can stop doing." Robby considered the question thoughtfully. "And there are places—not Strikersport, thankfully—where there's so much magic that if you can't keep it controlled, you'll implode, explode, and maybe turn everything around you inside out. The Monkey King—the version who chose you—comes from one of those places."

"Version?"

"The older Gods—the ones from the myths and stories—have a way of splitting as their followers split. That's why the Eight Immortals of Khaitan are similar to the ones in the rest of China but not exactly the same. It gets tricky. My mother and Chou understand better than me and Dad."

While Miss Frazier absorbed the information, Robby wondered if he should call his mother for help immediately. He still wasn't sure how much she knew or understood, but he didn't want to ask and find out, either. Besides, she'd said he was old enough to make his own decisions and live with them, hadn't she?

William joined Robby and Miss Frazier. "Can you call your mother?"

The request was annoying only because Robby had just decided not to. "I can help, you know."

"Can you tell what's wrong with Mr. Rogers, then?"

Embarrassed, because that was one area he wasn't useful for, Robby admitted, "No. I can't."

"Could you take him to her to examine? Not to mention ask her what to do about that cub you're carrying?" At Robby's expression, William grinned. "You wouldn't want to keep it from its parent, would you?" He patted the stone lion statue gently.

"No, I suppose not." It was a tribute to how sulky Robby felt that he didn't elaborate.

"Good. Miss Frazier, would you go with Robby? Mrs. McLeod might help you understand the situation better."

Mr. Andersen interrupted angrily. "Wait a minute. That young lady is our tour guide and she's supposed to take us to that charity banquet downtown tonight. And the show afterwards."

"My mother is catering that banquet," Robby pointed out, checking his watch. "She's bound to be there already. We could just go together."

When William hesitated, Gilly frowned thoughtfully and said, "I'm noticing a trend and I think keeping an eye on the Andersens would be a good idea. Just in case."

The Bostonian glared at Gilly furiously. "Are you implying—"

"Not implying a thing, old fellow, not a blessed thing. Outright saying. Trouble seems to be following you and your missus around today. What that means is subject to speculation, but I'm thinking it'd be a good idea to stay close, just in case." Gilly's accent shifted to a pure and near perfect Boston accent and back to his usual gruff tones with an ease Robby deeply admired. "Rosie here put a lot of time into setting up her charity banquet. I'd hate to see anything happen to it."

Rosamund simpered at Gilly. "It's so sweet of you to care, Officer Kenneth. Just for that, I may allow you to escort me after all. No matter what Mummy says."

Ignoring his cousin, William said, "I think you're right about keeping an eye on the Andersens. But it's far too early for the guests to arrive. Gilly, you and I, and Rosamund, can stay here and keep our guests entertained while Robby and Miss Frazier go ahead."

Robby agreed. "You're probably right. Can we use your car, though? I came up in the oodle-mobile of Mr. Rose's and you'll need it to get downtown with all these people."

"The—oodle-mobile?"

"Yeah. That's what they call lots of Good & Plenties, right?"

Stephanie tried not to giggle and failed. "It does look like a whole box of them, doesn't it?" she agreed.

"It does." Grinning, William handed Robby a key and took the bus key. "If it looks like Mr. Rogers needs medical aid, get him to a hospital first."

The advice was entirely unnecessary. "Teach me how to change an oil filter, while you're at it." Robby picked up Mr. Rogers, who was snoring softly and peacefully. "Come along, Miss Frazier. We'd better hurry. Ma's already having a busy day and she's not going to appreciate interruptions."

The banquet hall was owned by the Trendle family and located in what had been the largest and most expensive hotel in Strikersport before Jewel Island Resort had been built. Back in the day the city's train station—also a Trendle property—had come in beneath the elegantly designed building. Nowadays the station was no longer in use, airplanes having supplanted passenger trains. There'd been talk of putting in a subway, even some tunnels built, but work had halted during the war and never continued.

When the Trendles had focused more of their wealth on their media holdings, the hotel had been turned into a combination theater and entertainment center. There was a bar and a restaurant on the top floor and function space on the floor above the theater. Offices, including the radio station, took up the rest of the ten story building,

Right then the lobby was covered in ribbons and fake garlands of greenery. Robby's cousin Tse was hanging from the top of a ladder, tying one end of a garland to a peg, while other members of the catering company offered the girl unnecessary and undesired advice. She was telling them to shut up and stop bothering her as Robby and Miss Frazier arrived.

Before Robby could add his own advice to the mix, Tan, Grandfather Cheh's second-in-command and Mudan McLeod's chief assistant ap-

proached him. "Robby, do you have any reason to be bringing unconscious strangers here, instead of the hospital?" Tan looked calm as usual,
but Robby could tell this job had him a bit frazzled. Between having to
prepare one of Miss Rosamund's charity banquets and setting up the theater for the Fragrant Stone Players, he was being kept busy.

Robby jerked a thumb at the man he carried. "There's some trouble involving this gentleman. We need Ma's help. Is she in the kitchen?"

"She's in the banquet hall. Don't interrupt her for too long. We still have
a lot to do." Tan hurried off to stop someone from treating the decorations
like part of a lion dance. "This isn't New Years! Show some respect!" he
snapped. "Honestly, Cheung, we can't take you anywhere."

Robby ignored the confusion to head up the stairs, Miss Frazier trailing behind him. "What were you two saying?" she asked, and Robby realized he and Tan had automatically spoken in Chinese.

"Just finding out where my mother is hiding," Robby explained. "And
I'm not to interrupt her for too long, so we'd better hurry."

They avoided falling decorations and tumbling decorators before entering the banquet room. It was quieter here, for the decorations had already been put up and the only one left was Robby's mother. He paused at
the door, seeing her survey the room, her back to him. She was dressed in
pants and a work shirt right that moment. Later, once the party had begun,
she'd change to the fashionable *cheongsam* that gave a kind of authenticity
to her service.

"And what is it that brings you to me when I'm busy, First Born Son?"
Mudan didn't even need to turn to acknowledge his presence, but then she
was facing the oversized, gold-plated, wine bottle Harriet Krane had demanded they include in the decorations. She even spoke in English, having noticed Miss Frazier behind Robby.

"I have a gentleman here who may have something to do with the incident at the temple earlier." Robby didn't ask if Mudan already knew about
it. Chou had agreed to bring her the news, being better able to get around
quickly. Besides, he owed Robby after the mess he'd made of the resort's
bus. "You remember Aunt Hikaru mentioning some jewelry she'd failed
to acquire at an auction? He's wearing it. I think it let someone use him
as a tool. It might even be a ghost, but I'm not sure about that. They spoke
Khaitanese through him, though, and called me half-breed, so—"

Mudan turned, one eye twitching slightly as she glared at him. "Enough,
son. You need not prove to me that you are you. Put the man down and
I'll look at him."

Robby did so, keeping silent with some difficulty as his mother knelt beside Mr. Rogers and considered him thoughtfully. "If he was possessed as you suggest, he is no more. I do sense something, a mark on his spirit like a dirty fingerprint." She took the brooch Robby offered her, adding, "Batsu work, as Hikaru said. It appears to be broken, however."

Seeing the way his mother looked at him, Robby fidgeted nervously. "I—may have hit it a bit too hard."

Mudan sighed. "If it had power, it does no more. That doesn't mean the source is gone, however. Hikaru told me it was one of several pieces in a set stolen some time ago. From what I understand, they have been causing trouble wherever they turn up. How did this man act while he wore it?"

Miss Frazier answered before Robby could, "William—Mr. Jarvis— said the man was convinced he served justice somehow. That he might have some reason to hate Mr. Andersen; since he was trying to attack him with a *shi shi* statue Mrs. Andersen bought from Mrs. Krane." She paused, adding, "And why *shi shi* again?"

"An interesting question, but I'm not sure what you mean by again," Mudan said.

"This morning, when I went to ask Chou to help with the bus, Mrs. Andersen was complaining that he'd told her companion a statue at the Jeen Loon was of a—what was it—a fooey dog? Except it was a *shi shi* statue."

"*Fu* dog," Robby offered helpfully. "Which isn't really a thing in China. Or at least, the statues are lions, stone lions. There are dog breeds called *fu* dogs, and the name might—" He trailed off at his mother's expression and added, "Sorry."

Mudan shook her head and sighed. "What my son is long-windedly trying to say is that Chou would not have called a *shi shi* anything of the sort."

"I got that impression," Miss Frazier agreed. "He was really frustrated with Mrs. Andersen about it. I have a feeling she does that sort of thing often, to rattle cages and get things cheaper. Mr. Andersen seemed to think so, at least."

Talking about *shi shi* caused the little one in Robby's jacket to squirm, drawing Mudan's attention. Flushing, because he'd half-hoped to keep the creature, Robby took it out and handed it to her.

"A living stone statue?" Mudan cradled the *shi shi* cub in her hands gently. "This is a thing that belongs to Khaitan, not here. And its workmanship is familiar, more Batsu art."

" QUICK! FOLLOW ME. "

"Could it belong with that *shi shi* Mrs. Andersen bought?" Miss Frazier asked. "There should be something under its paw. And it came alive too."

"Really? How very interesting. But, no." Mudan stroked the cub's head. "That was a male *shi shi* and ought, properly, to be holding a ball. Where is your mother, little one?"

The cub mewled and Mudan was about to say more when she looked up sharply, glaring past Robby and Miss Frazier.

Without turning, Robby glanced into the reflection of the wine bottle and caught Miss Frazier by the arm, dragging her to the side as a big man in fine clothes rushed at them.

"Them again?" Miss Frazier asked plaintively and Robby guessed the thug was one of the Bear Gulch gang she and his brother had encountered earlier. "Why are they here?"

"At least it isn't Wugong," Robby grumbled, dodging another man. "I'm getting tired of centipedes, frankly."

The sharp sound of a gun being fired drew their attention towards the entrance and Robby froze. A half-dozen more finely dressed thugs were entering the room. "Ma, can you distract them so I can—"

"Young man, they have a few too many guns for you," Mudan pointed out. "And the same goes for you, too, young lady. Leave that pretty hairpin where it is, please."

"You can't expect me to—" Robby's protest faltered at the expression on Mudan's face.

"I can, and I do, expect you to behave sensibly, my child. Choose your battles wisely." Mudan eyed the obvious leader of the group, keeping her hands spread as she moved between Robby and their attackers. "You work for Mr. Horne, do you not? What is it you wish here?"

"We're supposed to take that guy there." The obvious leader pointed at Mr. Rogers. "That's all. Get out of the way and we'll do just that."

"And what is it you intend to do with him, once you have him?" Mudan asked.

"That's our boss's lookout, not yours, lady." The man eyed Mudan as he came closer, "Look, he's just a two-bit liar who caused the boss a bit of trouble. You don't need to worry about a con-tree-temms between folk like us, do you? You just let us take the guy and we'll leave you to your lovely little swa-ray."

"Or, alternatively," another voice said from behind the group, "You could make a noise like a kite and go away empty-handed. Trust me, it'll hurt a lot less."

The men turned, moving just far enough so Robby could see the rangy black-clad figure at the doorway. His eyes went wide with shock at the sight. The newcomer was dressed in a black trench-coat and wearing an old fedora, but that wasn't what startled him most. "Tiger?" he breathed, staring at the red mask disbelievingly.

Mudan put a hand to her face and grumbled, "I do not remember asking for your help, Tiger."

"But you get it anyway, Mrs. McLeod. Can't let thugs like these have their own way all the time. They get uppity." Tiger said gruffly. As the thugs raised their guns to fire at him, he swung a slim black cane, a beam of energy lancing out from its tip to melt the weapons' barrels. "Now, now. That's naughty of you. There's going to be a party here in an hour or so and we don't want to make a mess."

Robby slid his hand into his pocket, wondering if he could find an opportunity to help, but Mudan stopped him. "You and Miss Frazier get Mr. Rogers to safety. Take him, and this brooch, to your grandfather. He'll know what to do."

With a sigh, Robby took the brooch, even as Tiger leapt over several of their attackers, calling, "I'll make a path for you, young'un. Don't worry."

Grousing at Tiger's idea of humor, Robby slung Mr. Rogers over his shoulder again and gestured to the door at the back of the room. "Quick," he said. "Follow me."

Only when he'd gone too far to do anything about it did Robby realize Mudan still had the *shi shi* cub.

Knowing better than to take the grand staircase, Robby led Miss Frazier to the service stairs. He could hear fighting behind him and knew his mother's people were doing their part. He just hoped he could get his charges to safety so he could come back and help.

"I thought that Tiger fellow was a criminal," Miss Frazier said, glancing back over her shoulder as she pulled Sun Wukong's staff from her hair. "Why is he helping us?"

Robby forced himself to keep a straight face. "Tiger and Dragon don't like people horning in on their territory." Strikersport was supposed to be off-limits of course, but he supposed the masked man had cause, given the situation.

It was obvious Stephanie was too confused to argue. Of course, this had been a difficult day already, what with Monkey loaning her his staff and learning magic existed. Admittedly, Robby felt shaken, himself. He hadn't expected Tiger to show up.

They reached the stairwell by now and the sound of shouts echoed from below. "Damn," he muttered, peering over the railing. Horne had pulled out all the stops on this one. Robby could have gotten past this mess on his own, but escape was hampered by having both Mr. Rogers and Miss Frazier to worry about. At least Horne and his gang weren't sorcerers. That'd really put a damper on things.

Grimly, Robby headed upstairs and Miss Frazier asked, "Not that I'm arguing, but where are we going?"

"I can get help if we reach the radio tower," Robby told her. He didn't know how to explain that help to his companion and decided not to try. At least not yet. "Can you manage the steps? It's a few flights up and I don't think the elevator's safe. They might find a way to stop it and then we'd be trapped for real."

"I have to do a lot of walking," Miss Frazier countered. "I'll be fine. Just keep moving. And maybe save your breath for running instead of talking so much?"

Robby grinned, about to respond. Except Mr. Rogers moaned then and jerked around on Robby's shoulder. "Hey. Don't do that. You're safe."

"What happened? Where am I? Where's Athena? Who are you? Why—."

"I don't know exactly what happened to you," Robby answered quickly. "You're in the Trendle Tower. If Athena is Mrs. Andersen, she's still at the casino—I hope. I'm Robby McLeod and you're being hunted by a gang of thugs. Got any thoughts on why?"

The man struggled a moment more, too confused and muddled to really understand. Then he looked down and swallowed hard. "Oh God. Don't drop me. Please don't drop me."

"I'll try not to. It'll help if you stayed still."

The door opened ahead of them and three Chinese men stepped out on the landing. Robby might have sighed with relief, but he recognized the armbands worn by Wugong's men. He drew his chain-whip and switched on the energy field, tightening his grip on Mr. Rogers.

At the same time Miss Frazier took up a fighting stance she must have learned through Monkey's staff. Robby could tell it was guiding her. He could also see she was beginning to get a feel for what she needed to do. Without help she'd be lost, but it was obvious she was learning and learning fast.

"Give us the brooch," the biggest of the three newcomers ordered. "That's all we want."

"Brooch?" Mr. Rogers repeated. "That thing Athena gave me? Let them have it. It isn't important."

Robby thought about it, then shrugged. "Will you let us past if I give it to you?"

The man, a broad shouldered, heavy-set fellow Robby thought might be Northern Chinese, considered the question. "Of course, Westerner. We didn't come here for anything else."

Behind him, one of the others said in Cantonese "If he believes that, I have a mustard mine to sell him, too."

Pretending not to understand, Robby said, "Let us through and I'll give you what you're asking for." He returned his weapon to its pocket and drew out the brooch, holding it up for the men to see.

They stepped sideways and as Miss Frazier and Robby moved past them, one made a teasing grab at the young woman. That got him smacked in the forehead by the staff and Robby said, "You asked for that. Don't make her angry. She's got a mean streak. Besides, this is what you want, right?" He lifted the brooch again, so its gold and topaz surface sparkled in the light.

"That's it. Give it to us," their leader demanded.

"I have a better idea," Robby said, tossing the thing down the stairwell. "Go fetch."

The leader's mouth dropped open and he turned to look. Immediately, Robby seized the moment, kicking the man in the side, sending him reeling down the steps. Beside him, Miss Frazier gave the third man several gentle taps with Monkey's staff, in a way Robby knew was all her. Monkey didn't hesitate to crack skulls when the opportunity presented itself.

Still, it was enough to keep the fellow occupied and the second man, seeing his leader down for the count, made a quick decision between discretion and valor. He rushed down the stairs himself, yelling, "You'll pay for that!" as he went.

"Maybe," Robby muttered, "But not just yet, I hope. Come on, Miss Frazier. Let's get to the roof before someone else catches up."

The KPRT radio station was owned and operated by the Trendle family and its tower stood tall on the rooftop. The studio itself was down on the sixth floor, but the controls and equipment were in a little room right next to the antenna.

Setting Mr. Rogers down, Robby pulled out his keys and opened the door. "Don't worry, Miss Frazier. No one will be here to bother us," he said, noticing the worried look on her face. "Miss Trendle hired McLeod Motors to handle maintenance, so even if there were, they'd be a friend."

"What are you going to do?"

"Call for help," Robby told her, fiddling with the controls and resetting the frequency. "Now let's see, he's usually listening to 'Sunnyside' about this time. That helps."

"He?"

"You'll see," Robby reassured his companions. This wasn't really a thing he wanted to do, but he couldn't see a better way out of this trap at the moment. "Meng. Come to the station," he said into the microphone. "Emergency."

"Who's Meng?"

"You still haven't explained why I'm here," Mr. Rogers added.

"Mostly because I'm not sure how you got into this," Robby told the man. "What do you remember?"

"I was—talking—with Athena and she gave me—that thing you threw away." From the way Mr. Rogers spoke, Robby had a feeling his relationship with Mrs. Andersen was not particularly innocent. "I don't remember anything else."

Unsure if that meant Mrs. Andersen was another tool or an instigator, Robby said, "Just as well. You'll be a lot happier not knowing."

"He might be, but I'm not sure I will," Miss Frazier said. "Just what is going on?"

"We have too many fingers in one pie and it's getting messy," Robby answered. "Gong Gong—my grandfather—might be able to help."

Miss Frazier eyed him doubtfully. "Robby, just how are we going to get from here," she indicated the tower roof, then pointed towards Chinatown, "to there?"

"With a bit of help from an old friend." Robby scanned the landscape, trying to decide which way Meng would come. Inevitably, he was looking the exact wrong direction, because just as he focused on Chinatown's Dragon Gate a heavy silvery object wrapped itself around his neck and licked his ear.

"Damnit, Meng, don't do that!" Robby grumbled.

The dragon, currently no longer than his forearm and glittering in the late-afternoon sunset, grinned at him. Sensing its question, Robby told it, "We need help getting to Chinatown. Will you give us a ride, please?"

Behind him, Miss Frazier was making odd choked noises and Mr. Rogers was hyperventilating. Robby ignored the two in favor of 'listening' for the answer. "Yes," he agreed. "Five bowls of sweet and sour, three bowls of hot and sour and ten *cha siu bao*." Ordinarily he'd bargain, but this was an emergency and Meng knew he could name his price.

"That—that's—that—" Miss Frazier gasped.

"It's a dragon. Well, that's his favorite shape. I'll explain more, later." Robby glanced significantly at Mr. Rogers, wishing the man had had the decency to stay unconscious until they were properly safe.

"But—" Miss Frazier recovered herself enough to change her question to another, more sensible one. "How is it going to carry us. It's too— Oh. Never mind."

That last was because Meng, with his typical sense of humor, had chosen that moment to enlarge himself, spreading his form to extend some twenty or so feet. Robby made a mental note to speak long and pedantically to Meng's handler about the creature's manners. He gave Miss Frazier an apologetic grin, telling her, "Sorry. He likes to startle people, I'm afraid."

"I'm not riding that!" Mr. Rogers protested.

"Well, we could leave you," Robby said equably. "But those three just now weren't the only ones after you. And I'm not sure those other men cared more about that bauble of yours or you."

Mr. Rogers blanched. "I—I'll come with you."

After helping Miss Frazier onto Meng's back, Robby got Mr. Rogers settled as well and climbed up behind the pair. "Chinatown, Meng. As fast as you can go. And no—."

Meng swooped upwards and did a perfect Immelmann before leveling off to speed towards the mountain.

"—acrobatics," Robby sighed as Miss Frazier screeched and clung for dear life. If nothing else, Mr. Rogers had fainted again, which meant one less person to have to explain things to.

He just hoped his grandfather would understand.

Chapter Six
The Gold River Casino's Kitchens are Known for their Attention to Detail

Rosamund was bored. All the excitement and interest seemed over and since Gilly wouldn't get her anything from the bar, she didn't see a point to remaining. "Are we done here, yet?" she asked.

Gilly was busy picking up tables and putting things in order, a habit she found both mystifying and oddly endearing. She didn't understand the man at all but he had a way of making her feel like there was at least one stable point in the universe. She'd expressed that to him once, to his obvious amusement. "I could have someone take you to the banquet hall, if you'd like," he said. "Or home, if you'd rather."

"Mrs. McLeod doesn't like it when I come in too early. I don't know why. And it's boring at home."

"It's dangerous to be on your own right now," Gilly pointed out, eyeing her with an unfamiliar expression. "You don't know how to fight."

"I do too," Rosamund countered.

Gilly hefted her purse before handing it to her. "Swinging this thing—no matter how heavy—at people's heads doesn't count as fighting."

Turning to William, who was talking to that boring Mr. Andersen, Rosamund appealed to her cousin, "Billy, make Gilly stop picking on me. Isn't there something I can do?" She paused, adding, "Billy, Gilly! I made a rhyme!"

William covered his face with his hand. "Yes, cousin Rosamund. You did."

"Isn't it funny?"

"Hilarious, Rosamund. Just hilarious." William sighed. "You and Boopsie should go home. There isn't anything you can do here and we're too busy to entertain you."

Rosamund was about to gather her things and haughtily make an exit when several dozen elegantly suited men entered the room. They looked like the casino's security at first and she wondered what had taken them so long. It'd been at least half an hour since that silly *shi shi* statue came to life and scared everyone, after all.

These men, however, didn't seem right to Rosamund. Crogan's security always looked like they'd been stuffed into ill-fitting suits. These newcomers were perfectly and impeccably fitted out in outfits that might have been tailored for them. They weren't, her experienced eye could see that much. They just knew how to wear nice clothes properly, unlike most of Crogan's men.

More importantly, Rosamund spotted a familiar face towards the back of the group. She opened her mouth to speak, then discretion, rare and therefore a novelty with her, took hold. The man who'd called himself Jones and been the family butler for the last few weeks was too well dressed and too composed to be just a servant. Rosamund encouraged Boopsie to sit beside her and called out to Gilly, "You there. Boy. Bring me a cocktail. Right now."

Gilly started, then glanced at the men approaching Mr. Andersen and William. "Right away, Miss Krane," he said in the meekest of voices, obediently going behind the bar to pour a drink and bring it to her. "Is this to your liking?"

"I'd rather have a whiskey, but someone won't let me," Rosamund told him haughtily, sipping the sparkling water and cranberry juice. Then she whispered, "Mummy was right about Jones, wasn't she?"

"Seems so," Gilly agreed, giving Boopsie a bit of sausage from the hors d'oeuvre tray. "I'll warn Billy." The last was said with that quirky smile that meant he thought he was being droll and Rosamund grinned at him despite the tension Jones' sudden appearance roused in her.

Watching the men approach, Rosamund wasn't surprised when Jones took over. The butler, or whatever he was, was obviously a leader. "Well now, I appear to have come at a bad time." He offered his hand, adding, "It's been quite some time since we last met, Mr. Andersen. I'm Horne, of Bear Gulch Real Estate. I believe we have an appointment. I hope you don't mind my showing up early, but we've had a number of interesting problems come up today and I'm needed elsewhere all too soon."

Oblivious to the way everyone else in the room, including his wife and her companion reacted, Mr. Andersen said, "At last, Mr. Horne. I've been quite looking forward to meeting with you." He turned to look at William, "This is a private matter."

Rosamund recognized a dismissal when she heard one and so did William. Without an excuse to argue, William agreed. "We'll wait for you downstairs, then."

"I don't think Jones is his real name, Boopsie," Rosamund muttered as they left.

"I don't either," Boopsie told her with a serious look. "He smells like he's lying all the time, mommy."

"I agree, Boopsie," Gilly said, petting Rosamund's dog on the head. "He smells like trouble."

William groaned as he walked ahead of them. "I wish you two wouldn't do that."

"Don't be offended, Boopsie. It's not your fault Billy can't understand you."

"That's all right, mommy. I know. Most people can't."

"Truth to tell," Gilly admitted, "I'm not sure I'm understanding him either. Not the way you are, at least."

That made William stop and turn, looking at all three of them with a strange expression. "Gilly, are you telling me—"

They all looked back at him with what Rosamund knew were identically innocent expressions and Gilly said, "If you're asking if Boopsie really answers her when she talks to him, the answer's 'yes, sort of'. I'm not sure if she's translating it to talk talk in her head or if she really hears him, though. Never have worked that part out."

William sighed. "Are you sure Strikersport isn't the sort of place that attracts magic and weird things?"

"Well, it wasn't back in the day." Gilly's grin was pure mischief. "I think that's changing, though. Once you start fiddling around with rifts and magic and mixing them up, things can get tricky. Add a few Gods and Immortals to the mix and all bets are off."

They were just reaching the end of the staircase and about to round the corner when someone shouted ahead of them. "Hey, you can't go that way—" A sound like someone getting punched followed and William stopped them from taking another step.

"I smell trouble, mommy," Boopsie told Rosamund. "I don't think I like this."

Looking at Boopsie, William said, "I don't think I need a translation for that. Gilly, I want you to get Rosamund and Boopsie somewhere safe."

"I don't need protection," Rosamund objected.

"Yes, you do," Gilly answered and Boopsie agreed. "A purse won't help against a gang of thugs trying to make trouble." He took Rosamund's hand, his fingers unexpectedly warm. "I don't want you hurt, Rosie. Go on. Billy, I'll take care of her. You go do what you have to."

Before Rosamund could object, or pull free, Boopsie caught her other hand in his teeth and gently pulled her back. She could have slipped free easily, but she honestly had no idea how to help.

Leaving William behind, they headed upstairs again. "I don't think Mr. Horne will be pleased to see us," Rosamund objected as they returned to the Pacifica Hall.

"I'm sure he won't. But there's nowhere else to go." Gilly eyed the men guarding the area where Horne and Mr. Andersen talked. Intent on their discussion—which was obviously to neither's liking—the two men didn't notice Rosamund or Gilly at all.

Realizing the men might try to throw them out, Rosamund said loudly and in a pouting sort of way, "I want another drink. Boopsie, stop pulling me. I'm thirsty and I haven't had a proper whiskey in ages. Because this mean man keeps taking them away."

Gilly eyed her and smiled ruefully. "I do. Because you've been making yourself sick on them. And you know once you've started you can't stop."

All that was true and part of their usual conversation, but it had the effect of making the four men guarding Horne relax. Rosamund was almost sure they moved their hands away from their guns, deciding she wasn't a threat.

"What the devil is all that noise?" Mr. Andersen demanded. He got to his feet and tried to push his way past Horne's men. "Hey, let me through."

"Now Mr. Andersen, we haven't finished our talk." Horne jumped to his feet.

"I believe I've made my position clear, Horne. It's taken me ten years to track you down. I expect you to return the items you swindled from me immediately. Until then, there's nothing more to say. What right do your men have to try and hold me?"

"No legal right at all," Horne said in what might have been a reassuring way if he hadn't followed it up with, "Of course, the law and I aren't always on the best of terms anyway. Are we, Officer Kenneth?" Horne stepped between his men to eye Gilly with a broad and nearly perfect smile. A gold tooth, set with a small ruby, gleamed in his mouth. It was supposed to show his wealth, but it looked more like he hadn't brushed his teeth lately.

Gilly eyed the man thoughtfully. "Figured you'd recognize me," he admitted. "I am a bit noticeable."

Now that was true, Rosamund agreed. "But he looks ever so much better in a suit than he does in a police uniform," she said, and got a quick and appreciative grin from Gilly for her attempt to distract the man. It worked, too, for Horne turned to look at her sharply. "Better than you ever did in your butler suit, in fact."

"Your mother spoils you, girl. You and that brother of yours," Horne said. "I was never so glad to be fired than I was this morning."

Mr. Andersen stared at the man blankly. "Wait. Fired? Butler? You're a common laborer now?" he mocked.

"There's nothing common about me, you upper-class twit." Horne sneered. "Sitting so sweet and pretty on your velvet throne trying to cheat me out of my share of our treasure? Did you think I wouldn't notice you bringing your little friends into my territory to play?"

That made Gilly raise a brow. "Your territory?" he repeated and Rosamund noted he was moving sideways, away from her. "Correct me if I'm wrong, but I'm almost certain your territory is over in Bear Gulch. Not here in Strikersport. Unless you're telling me you're not the boss of the Bear Gulch Syndicate."

"Bear Gulch Syndicate?" Mr. Andersen laughed derisively at the news. "You've become a common criminal? A mere thug? You were a brilliant mineralogist, Horne. I thought you and I could partner again, but obviously not. This meeting is over!"

While Rosamund reflected that her brother and Mr. Andersen had the same thickheaded and stubborn inability to read the situation, Horne ignored the man to walk up to Gilly and stare down at him, sneering. "You know, I'm thinking you're a bit too smart for your own good, little man."

"Not really." Gilly moved a step further away, giving Rosamund a warning glance when she tried to join him. "Or I'd have realized there were more than just two gangs working here a good deal earlier."

"Gangs?" Mr. Andersen demanded. "What gangs?"

"Shut up, Andersen," Horne snapped. "More than two?"

"At least three, maybe four, unless I miss my count." Gilly looked thoughtful. "Your lot, some outside talent from Boston, the Centipedes— And maybe another group besides that? I'm not sure."

"Do go on."

Gilly gestured towards Horne's men. "Your men dress fancy, because you like them to pretend to be quality. You never hire anyone who can't be made to look the clean cut American dream. Just like the group that kidnapped Mrs. Andersen. The ones Maloney and I fought back at *Chiming Temple* were too ragtag to be yours; they all had Boston accents, anyway. As for Wugong's Centipedes, it's pretty obvious you don't have anything to do with them."

"Centipedes? Wugong? Who the devil is he when he's at home?"

"Oh do stop interrupting, Mr. Andersen," Rosamund snapped, tired of the man's inability to recognize danger. "Boopsie and I want to know what's going on."

"Really, I don't care, mommy," Boopsie told her, eyes intent on Horne. His lip was curled back from his canines and he looked ready to pounce any minute.

"That's all right, dear. I quite understand. But I think this is important." She could tell her dog was ready to act as soon as action was necessary, but for the life of her, she wasn't sure what the best move would be. She did wish Gilly would stop moving away from her. She didn't like the way Horne looked at him.

"All of you shut up and stop interrupting," Horne growled angrily. "Well, I won't say you're wrong, Officer Kenneth. It hardly matters, of course, but you are, in fact, quite correct. Andersen's men have been coming into Bear Gulch recently and poking their nose in my business. So, obviously, I had to do something to explain to him just how little I appreciate his efforts."

"*MY* efforts?"

"Shut him up, boys," Horne snapped, not bothering to look back at Andersen. Two of his men turned, grabbing the older man by the elbows and giving him a sucker punch that left him gasping and wheezing on the ground. "We'll be taking him and his—ladies—with us. The girl too. Not the dog. We don't need a 'talking' dog. Or whatever little miss out of her mind thinks he is."

"Rosie, Boopsie, run!" Gilly shouted, "Get help!" At the same time he threw a punch at Horne that knocked the man to the floor.

Though she desperately wanted to fight, Rosamund knew her purse wasn't up to the job. She kicked her heels off and raced out of the room, Boopsie close beside her. Gunfire behind her made her flinch, but she didn't look back. Gilly had given her the chance she needed to escape and she took it.

She just hoped she could find someone to stop Horne before he did some real damage. Not that he could hurt Gilly. No one could hurt Gilly, she was absolutely certain of that much.

Rosamund found her cousin wrapping up the fight downstairs. Between the casino's security and the police—who must have arrived after she'd left—the mess looked like something no longer needing his help. She hurried up to him.

"I thought I told you to hide," William grumbled, glaring at Rosamund as if he thought it'd change her mind. Not that it ever had before.

Ignoring her cousin's annoyance, Rosamund told him quickly, "Well, you did, but the only place was back in the Pacifica Hall and that man, Mr. Horne, isn't very nice at all."

William stopped and looked at Rosamund. He was well versed in her euphemisms and he quickly took her meaning. "What is he doing?"

"He's had those men of his beat up that annoying Mr. Andersen. And I'm quite sure we heard gunfire when Boopsie and I left. Didn't we, Boopsie?"

"I'm not sure what it was, Mommy. It was loud and I didn't like it."

"And I don't blame you in the slightest," Rosamund told Boopsie, petting him gently. He could handle most situations but loud noises weren't his favorite at all. "Gilly sent me back down to get you. Well, to get help, but I know he meant you."

Already hurrying towards the stairs, William ordered, "You stay here, cousin. You lot, come along."

"As if you'll do anything of the sort," Boopsie said, looking up at Rosamund expectantly.

"Naturally not, Boopsie." Rosamund told her dog, following behind grimly. She didn't believe Gilly was in danger but the little niggling doubtful part of her, the part that knew the people who actually cared about her always went away, gnawed at her heart and made her afraid.

The scene in the Pacifica Hall didn't make Rosamund feel any better. There were bullet holes in the walls and while two of Horne's men were unconscious on the ground, neither he, nor the Andersens, were still there. Nor was Gilly, though there was a blackened and bloody handprint on the wall. A charred trail led towards the door behind the bar.

"I smell fire," Boopsie told her. "Gilly's fire. And centipedes. I don't like those centipedes."

Trying not to panic, Rosamund asked, "Is he hurt?"

"Is who hurt, and what are you doing following me when I told you to stay downstairs?" William turned around and Rosamund found herself the center of attention in a way she didn't like.

"Gilly. Is Gilly hurt? Boopsie says he smells his fire, whatever that means. And I'm not staying behind when Gilly might be in danger."

William stared at her. "For God's sake, cousin. You can't help him."

"No. He needs me. I know he does." She wasn't at all sure how she knew, just that she did. "Did they go downstairs that way, then?"

"Will you let me worry about it?" William demanded. "You stay here. I mean it."

"I will not. If I have to get into the kitchens the other way I will. Don't you dare try to stop me, William Jarvis. Not when I know Gilly needs me."

"ROSE—" William started to shout, but something in her expression made him calm down. "Cousin, I just don't want you hurt and neither would Gilly."

"That's fine. But I don't want Gilly hurt either and I think he already has been." She pointed at the bloodstain. "That's his, isn't it?" She didn't know why it looked seared and she didn't care.

With a sigh, William beckoned to a couple of the police officers. "You two, stay with her. If there's more gunfire or any other sort of danger, you get her out of here. And her little dog, too."

Boopsie grumbled, "That's a lame joke, mommy. Tell him it's a lame joke."

They followed the trail through the back halls and while the blood drops never got bigger than a pencil width, and a few handprints, they never disappeared entirely either. Worse, at least as far as Rosamund was concerned, there were little charred centipedes covering the floor. She remembered those only too well and knew what they could do.

When Rosamund pointed the insects out, William told her, "I was really hoping you wouldn't mention them."

"Well, that's the same thing that man who tried to steal our *tao tie* vase threw at Boopsie. Is it him again? And how did he do it, anyway?"

"I'm not entirely sure," William said, glancing at his men. "I'd rather not talk about it right now."

"Is it like all those silly—persons—who attacked my charity ball last year? The ones made of wood?"

"I think those were built by science," William muttered, then groaned as he added, "I told you, I don't want to talk about it right now."

"I think it's magic. It smells like magic," Boopsie offered.

"Now don't be silly, Boopsie. I keep telling you, magic is all smoke and mirrors." The look on William's face made Rosamund pause, "Isn't it?"

"Later, cousin. Please."

Rosamund sighed and went quiet. They were getting close to Gilly, she was sure of that much, and she could hear the sound of angry shouts somewhere ahead of her. That and Gilly's voice saying, "You really don't want—to open—that rift." He chuckled, a frighteningly weak sound, add-

" THE BLOB STRETCHED OUT, WRAPPING AROUND THE SNAKE... "

ing, "Definitely shouldn't have— Oh dear. This isn't going to be good."

They stepped into a large storeroom and Rosamund stared, deciding Boopsie was right about magic after all. How else to explain the swirling disc of purple-black at the center of the room. How else to explain the man flattened in the wall? How else to explain the strange monstrous beings struggling to reach Horne, their long blue robes billowing every time they hopped?

Scanning the fight, Rosamund saw no sign of Gilly. Horne's gang crouched in the center of the purplish black stuff, protected from the things and people trying to get at them. There were the two gangs Gilly had mentioned: the ruffians from Boston, Centipede man and his gang, as well as a woman commanding monstrous human figures in fine blue Mandarin robes. Yet there was something, a shadowy, smoky, movement in the darkness around them that made her feel oddly safe.

"Oh no," William said incomprehensibly as he stared. "Not another body stuck in the nth dimension."

"Where's Gilly?" Rosamund asked, not interested in his troubles. "Boopsie? Do you see Gilly?"

"I'm sorry, mommy. I smell him, but I don't see him."

"Gilly! Where are you?" Rosamund had to be forcibly restrained from moving forward. At the same time, more men in Chinese robes, their teeth bloody and their eyes empty, blocked her path. They hopped in place, giggling to themselves, while the woman stood behind them, raising and dropping a fan.

Horne said, "Wugong. You're as annoying as the Golden Dragon himself. Now you've made me lose that dingleberry and his women."

"He paid me to do it. Paid good money, too." The man with the centipedes, Wugong, spread his hands, his bugs swarming around the purple-black glow. "Besides, my partner has business with him."

"Did he pay you enough to deal with this?" Horne gestured behind him with something that looked like a Geiger counter. His men screamed, as the glow engulfed them, covering them entirely. They went silent a moment later, twisting together into an amorphous mass that reached out for Wugong and grasped him tightly.

The mass would have dragged the man into the void, kicking and shouting all the way, but for a huge snake formed of black smoke and stinking like a volcano. Squirming out of the shadows, it chomped down, ripping out a huge mouthful and sending a human figure flying against the wall.

The blob stretched out, wrapping around the snake, eliciting a cry of pain Rosamund knew despite his change. "Gilly?" she breathed. At the same time more blobs broke free of the darkness, one enveloping the woman. Immediately the strange hopping figures disappeared and the blobs moved towards William.

There was a noise behind Rosamund and looking back, she realized the *shi shi* statue had followed them down the stairs. It slipped between the frightened police officers and moved to block the thing attacking William. Her cousin's eyes went wide as it lashed out, protecting him from his attacker.

"I serve you in this, chosen of the Black Eagle," the *shi shi* said and William just stared, wild-eyed at it. "Command me."

It took Boopsie telling Rosamund, "I don't think he understands, mommy," for her to realize why her cousin wasn't taking advantage of the animal. "You'd better tell him."

"He says he's your servant. Something about a Black Eagle," Rosamund told William helpfully. "You'd better ask him to do something about that blobby thing. I'm not sure Gilly can handle it all by himself."

"Thanks for the vote of confidence, Rosie dear," Gilly shouted, twisting and struggling against several more of the blobs. "I really could use a bit more faith in my strength over here."

William sighed. "If you can do something about those—whatever they are—I'd appreciate it."

The lion bowed, a bit like Boopsie did when he wanted a treat, and leapt into the fight.

The battle was lit by flashing lights and accompanied by so many crashes and screams that Boopsie was terrified. He cowered in Rosamund's skirts and she dropped to her knees to embrace him protectively. He hated thunder most of all and while this wasn't a real storm, it was just as noisy and just as scary. Or so he kept telling her.

"Gilly! You have to make this stop," Rosamund shouted over the noise. "You're scaring Boopsie!"

The room shuddered as the snake, as Gilly, twisted and struggled against the things wrapped around him. "Doing my best here, Rosie my love. There's only so much one monster can do!" As the *shi shi* grasped a tendril of blackness in his mouth and tugged, Gilly added, "Even with help."

Annoyed at his excuses, Rosie snapped, "Nonsense. Don't be lazy. I know you can do better than that."

Tearing himself free of the tendrils, just enough to slither forward and stick his face in front of Rosamund, Gilly asked, "Really? Do you really think that?" There was that eager note to his voice she sometimes noticed when he needed encouragement.

Tentatively, because he really was very hot, she patted him on the tip of his nose. "Silly Gilly. Oh, another rhyme! Of course I do. You're just lazy when no one needs anything. But I need you right now. So you go give those bastards what for and send them packing for me. All right?"

Gilly whooped and swooped backwards, arching himself over the blobs and using his fangs to pull those trapped inside the tendrils free, tossing them, one by one, over to William and his men. At the same time the *shi shi* used the distraction to get behind Horne and knock the device he held from his hands. Immediately, the swirling disc heaved and twisted, enveloping the man and his men.

With a panicked shout, Gilly flung himself at the blackness and wrapped himself around it, transforming entirely to a cloud of sooty ash that filled the room and blinded everyone. When it cleared, the black glow was gone, along with Horne himself. His remaining men—those not already under arrest—were tossed around the room. Some were groaning and struggling to sit up, but one or two didn't look like they'd sit up again ever. Wugong and the woman were gone as well, though Rosamund wasn't sure if they'd escaped or been dragged into the void to their doom.

The *shi shi* moved towards William, but Rosamund was more worried about the man sprawled against one shelf, clutching his belly and gasping for air. "Gilly!" She ran over to him, Boopsie right behind her. "What's wrong. Are you hurt? You can't be hurt."

"I can too be hurt," Gilly gasped. "I'm not a God. And that was a lot of bullets for one retired monster to take."

"You're you," she told him, wiping his sweat-stained forehead with her handkerchief. "You'll be all right. I know you will."

Gilly raised his eyes to her, a purple-black glow shining in their depths. "Really? Truly? Are you sure about that? You'll be stuck with me if you're not careful."

As if she wasn't already stuck with him. "Who else would keep me entertained?" she demanded, helping him straighten up and—when he seemed ready—to stand.

With a chuckle, Gilly kissed her forehead, "Blessings, child. I think the feeling's mutual."

Before Rosamund could think of a suitable retort, William interrupted. "Er, cousin? Now you've got Gilly up on his feet, could you give me a hand here? Seeing as how you're the only one who seems to understand this *shi shi*?" The animal stared at him expectantly.

Going over to join her cousin, Rosamund asked the *shi shi*, "Do you need something?"

"Tell the Black Eagle's surrogate my child needs me. I must have his permission to go."

Child? That was right. The baby *shi shi* had been squirming around in Robby's jacket when he'd left with Miss Frazier. "He wants to look for that *shi shi* cub Robby took. But you have to give permission."

William eyed the *shi shi*. "You know the one who took it doesn't want to hurt it, right?"

"I know she is far from me and frightened. I will not hurt what does my baby no harm, but I must find her," the *shi shi* answered and Rosamund translated.

With a sigh, obviously worried that he was letting another problem loose on Strikersport, William said, "Go then. Just be careful."

As the *shi shi* ran off, William turned to his men. "We'll discuss what happened later. I don't want anyone talking about it until then. For now, get these men to jail and start working out who's doing what to whom. Before this mess gets any worse." Which, Rosamund thought wryly, was already too late.

"Anything you want me doing, boss?" Gilly asked.

"I think so. Go to Cheh Chang and see if he's willing to help out with this mess. I have a feeling we're going to need everyone we can get. Tell him I'm going to go to see his son-in-law, since it looks like we've got another rift device to deal with."

Gilly grinned. "Can I take the—what was it Robby called it—the oodle-mobile?"

"If you don't mind being seen in that thing, I don't care. Now get moving." William tossed Gilly the keys and turned back to his job.

Rosamund followed Gilly quietly, unwilling to let him out of her sight. She didn't know what was coming or what she could do about it, but she knew he needed her around and that was all that mattered. She just hoped Mr. Chang wouldn't mind uninvited guests.

Chapter Seven
Trendle Hotel's Train Station is no Longer in Operation

Chou cracked a rolling pin over the head of the Centipede thug who'd invaded the kitchen. "This is no place for bugs," he said firmly. "Go away. What do you people think this is? Grand Central station?"

Behind him, Mao—no fighter—was blocking the path of one of the nicely dressed thugs Chou had fought back in Chinatown. "I don't believe they understand, Chou. Otherwise they'd know better than to start a fight around hot oil." That last was because the thug had managed to knock Mao's wok to the floor, covering himself with its contents; a spicy dish of pork and tofu. The man was hopping around angrily, yelling in pain from the heat.

"It's not the flames, but the spice, that gets you," Chou said in English, presenting the man with his own personal goose-egg. "That and the thump to the noggin. So very sorry."

Their attackers unconscious, Chou looked at his friend. "Can you tie them up? I'd better check on Ma." From the sound of it, the entire building was under attack. He could hear police sirens in the distance, but he doubted they'd be able to do much, given how many people were involved.

"Go ahead. I can keep out of trouble, I think." Mao waved him on, using some spare aprons to tie the pair up. "I wonder, would anyone be interested in long pig?"

"No, Mao. No." Chou shook his head at his friend and hurried out the door, slipping past the fights and cursing the lack of a private spot. He urgently needed a quiet moment and he wasn't getting one. Then he remembered the radio studio's offices were tucked away towards the back of the first floor. All he needed were a few seconds alone.

As Chou entered the office, though, he was startled by a sudden wave of black shadowy smoke that chilled him to the bone. Then it backed off and a man stepped through the shadows, saying, "No, that's not one of them. Stop that. How does Ba She put up with you lot?"

Looking at the shadows, Chou recognized them immediately. Like their true master, they were tall and slim, with dozens of long, skinny, braids. Though barely dimensional black silhouettes, they shared the White Serpent's aquiline profile and characteristic self-confident air. One bowed to Chou apologetically and he bowed back before telling Simon. "Ba She doesn't mind their foolishness because it amuses him. But how did you end up with the White Serpent's Eight Shadows?"

"I only have four, thank the Gods," Simon grumbled, glaring at the figures flattening themselves against the wall and dancing mockingly. "And I have no idea why they're here. They just showed up out of nowhere. Good thing, too. More of Wugong's thugs were in here, wanting me to get them onto the roof. Damned if I know why." He waved at the ground behind him, where half a dozen members of the Centipede gang lay, simultaneously beaten and chilled into submission. None dared move a muscle, Chou noticed.

"I wouldn't know why either," Chou admitted. "But I don't think it's safe to stay here."

"I daresay you're right. Where were you headed?"

Chou gave up on finding any privacy. Simon was a bit too smart and a bit too curious to evade easily. "Upstairs to find my mother. I want to be sure she's alright. I only stopped here because I heard noises."

"I'll join you. I think this bunch is done playing for the moment." Simon gestured at his unasked for companions and added, "All right, you nuisances. Come along."

"You can tell me how you wound up with them while we go," Chou suggested, leading the way.

Simon told his side of the story quickly, with occasional interruptions from the invaders. Most of it wasn't new; Robby had told Chou about the fight in the temple and how Ba She had helped. What he didn't understand, and Simon couldn't explain, was who all these strangers were and why they were suddenly showing up and causing trouble.

There appeared to be at least three separate groups involved. There was the Bear Gulch gang who'd kidnapped Mrs. Andersen. Then there was that bunch Tiger had faced in the temple; east coast thugs by their accents. Last were the Centipedes, led by Hoshi's uncle Wugong and his partner. Robby had said he'd heard the woman speak in Batsu, a dialect of Khaitanese spoken by a small village in the Taklamakan desert. A secretive and private people, Chou only knew about them because so much of their replica work found its way onto the market. Now why would a woman of the Batsu be working with a criminal like Wugong?

"I knew our Immortals statues were broken," Chou told Simon as they hurried upstairs. "And someone mentioned Ba She's warning. But I didn't realize it's spilled over into the main city like this. Does this Andersen fellow have something to do with it? He and his wife keep turning up."

"I'm not sure. Andersen's a cagey fellow and his wife is—strange. She's obsessed about getting hold of some *shi shi* cub statue." Simon punched one of the Bear Gulch gang in the nose. "Frankly, they seem too good to be true."

"Good?" Chou repeated, disbelievingly. "I didn't meet Mr. Andersen, but I had to deal with his wife and she's—" He stopped himself. His mother didn't like him using that sort of language about people, even if they were annoying self-absorbed gits. "Let's just say she isn't a very nice lady."

"I believe you're understating the case. And that's part of the problem. Can anyone be that oblivious to the reactions of the world around them?"

Chou admitted that he'd never met anyone quite so unaware. "You think she does it to get her way, then?"

"Maybe. Or maybe they're neither of them what they seem." Simon was about to say more, but they had to fight their way past a knot of Centipedes and a group of poorly dressed thugs. By the time they'd passed, they'd reached the entrance to the banquet hall, where the fighting was at its worst.

All three gangs were there, caught up in a grand free-for-all. Chou's first thought was his mother would be furious when she found all her work ruined. Given, of course, she didn't know already.

Chou's concerns faded as a a trench-coated figure in a fedora rushed past him, swinging a stick that lit up from the end and knocked several Centipede gang-members to the ground. "Tiger?" he breathed, surprised at the change in the masked man's costume. What had happened to his hooded longcoat?

Then Chou's eyes went so wide he thought they'd fall out, as another black clad figure, this one in a voluminous robe concealing their body and hands entirely. "Dragon?" The blue mask certainly belonged to that particular vigilante, but he'd swear the person inside was someone entirely different. The impish part of him reacted before he could stop himself and he called out, "Dragon! I'm your biggest fan! Can I have an autograph?"

Dragon, or whomever it was, spun round, dodging attackers and sending them flying with a wave of their fan. "Quickly, take this and get out of here. Get it to safety!" a husky voice said. That, at least, was Dragon's voice, but he knew it couldn't be. Something flew through the air and he caught it automatically. A *shi shi* statue, almost the same as the one Chou had sold to Mrs. Andersen that morning. To his shock, he realized it was carved of living marble. It whimpered and he cradled it protectively in his hands.

Seeing Chou hesitate, Dragon glared at him, a look that made him turn and run out the door again, Simon close behind. He wasn't at all surprised when half the men in the banquet hall followed suit.

"I don't suppose you know why she gave that to you—and isn't Dragon a man?"

"Last I checked, he was. Why do you think he's a girl all of a sudden?"

Simon sounded thoughtful as he punched a man trying to grab the *shi shi* statue from Chou. "Well, if that wasn't a girl, Dragon's gotten a lot shorter and a bit curvier than he used to be."

Chou considered the possibilities. "Well, he is a sorcerer," he said finally, running into the kitchen. Mao was gone, as were the two men he and Chou had knocked out, leaving the steamed sticky rice rolls unprotected from Simon's companions. Shadows hid the tray from sight as they passed, transforming the things to empty air in seconds.

"Hey!" Chou protested. "Those were for the banquet. Ma'll be mad at you."

"Sorry," Simon apologized, "I can't do a thing with this lot."

Fortunately, the threat of his mother convinced the shadows to leave the food alone, Chou went to the freezer and brought out one of the smaller ice sculptures; the horse little Tse had painstakingly carved and painted with food coloring. "Here we are," he said. "This is perfect. Now you sit still for a moment, okay? Don't worry. This won't hurt a bit."

As Chou set the sculpture down beside the *shi shi* cub, Simon asked, "Er, dare I ask what you're going to do? You can't hide that thing in the freezer. It's the first place they'll look."

Chou grinned and put one hand on the *shi shi* cub and the other on the ice sculpture. "True," he agreed. "But they're looking for a marble baby *shi shi*." He exerted his magic, closing his eyes and imagining the swoops and twists of his spell. "Not a carved ice horse."

The energy swirled around his fingers and entered the statue, reshaping it from a terrified little *shi shi* cub to a rather amateurish ice carving of a horse, its limbs dyed pink and green and its body rearing as it kicked thin air. The ice sculpture changed in turn, taking on the appearance of the *shi shi* cub. Taking several deep breaths, and a sticky rice roll, Chou turned and grinned at Simon, who was staring, wide-eyed at him.

Finally the man said, "I thought you might be a sorcerer. Another illusionist?"

"I'll have you know my magic is transformative," Chou replied haughtily, skritching the chilly ears of the *shi shi* turned horse. He paused, frowning, and added, "How did you know I'm a sorcerer?"

Simon looked at him thoughtfully. "Oh, no reason. Just a suspicion I've had for a bit." He shrugged, "Never mind that. What do we do now?"

Chou was better at evading and reacting to trouble than he was at planning how to get out of it. "I don't suppose you have any ideas?"

"You could hide it in the freezer now."

"I think that Dragon fellow would be annoyed with me. I'm supposed to protect it. Besides, it'd be lonely."

Simon eyed the thing as it sat on its haunches and panted nervously. "If it's been turned to ice, won't it melt?"

"No. There are limits. I've reshaped and recolored its base substance. I can't make it not be marble."

Somewhere outside in the hall, a woman shouted, "Where is my *fu* dog?" Chou flinched. Mrs. Andersen still couldn't remember the right term.

Hearing her, Simon asked, "That means the other statue will melt, right?"

"Probably. Well, yes."

"Put it back in the freezer, leave the door ajar and let's make a run for it. We might escape through the station downstairs before someone notices."

It wasn't a choice Chou liked, but it seemed the only one possible at the moment. He just hoped he could keep Simon from realizing too much.

The two dozen men pursuing Chou and Simon fought amongst themselves as they ran. Luckily so, Chou thought. They would have caught up easily, otherwise. Even so, the sound of their pounding feet and curses echoed in the shadowy tunnels. They were getting closer.

The old train station had a tunnel leading into the hillside under Strikersport. Once upon a time, it'd been a beautifully decorated entry point into the Trendle hotel. Now it was abandoned, its tunnel dark and smelling of rust and unpleasant things.

Realizing they'd never escape at this rate, Chou searched for a certain disused door. The light from their flashlights, borrowed from the kitchen's utility room, picked out rust, rats and debris. At last he spotted the faint line in the wall that marked the spot.

"Where are you going? Shouldn't we get out of here?"

Chou sighed. "This is another way out. If your friends can keep it hidden once we're through, those bastards won't know to follow us." He worked at the door, deliberately making it look harder to open than it was. At the same time he scraped his foot against the wall, making it shriek like rusted metal on metal.

"I don't know about this—"

Grabbing Simon by the arm, Chou pulled him through and closed the door behind them. "Never mind. Just have your shadow friends cover it up. We'll try sneaking outside once they've passed."

Simon complained as he obeyed, "They'll hear that noise and come back."

"Maybe, maybe not." Chou leaned against the door, feeling the chill of Ba She's servants as they passed him. The White Serpent was the Immortal who guided the underground river in the southern part of Khaitan and he could smell that cavern's cool dank stone. It made a pleasant change from the stink of rust and rotten food.

At last Simon said, "They're gone. I just wish I knew what was going on."

Chou agreed. "This day has been difficult enough as it is. They're all outsiders, but I can't figure out what they want. Aside from causing trouble."

"Ba She mentioned the Feast of Hungry Ghosts, which should be starting soon. It was getting dark outside when those Centipedes crawled their way into the station's office." Simon's face, just visible in the lamplight, had a puzzled, thoughtful look. "How many are there, you think?"

"Aside from my mother's people, who belong here, there were at least three groups. The Centipedes, Horne's 'Gentlemen' from Bear Gulch and some others I don't recognize." The last were the ones from the temple.

"Could they work for Crogan?"

That was unlikely. Crogan had himself a pretty sweet deal in Strikersport and part of that deal involved keeping his greedy mitts out of Chinatown. The gangster—supposedly reformed—knew from experience just how much trouble arguing with Cheh Chang could cause. Chou didn't say so, knowing he'd have to explain how he knew such things. Instead he offered, "I think they sounded more East Coast, myself."

"Leading us straight back to Andersen. Again." Simon sighed. "I checked out the newspaper morgue for old articles about him. All I could get was that he's old money. Some of it comes from his mining company, the rest he made by buying up art from people escaping the war."

That didn't surprise Chou. An unscrupulous buyer could make a killing off desperate refugees. Nor was he surprised when Simon added, "Mrs. Andersen and her sister, Minerva, also collect Chinese sculptures and jewelry."

"So they are sisters?" Chou asked. "That sort of white woman all look alike to me."

Simon chuckled. "In this case, there's a reason. They're twins." He was about to say more when he paled, turning towards the doorway with a frightened expression. "Dear God. What is that?"

Unnerved by Simon's expression, Chou looked as well, though all he could see was the battered metal of the door itself. "What? What are you seeing?" He corrected himself, "What are your shadow friends seeing?"

One of those shadows flowed up in front of Chou, coalescing and changing from Ba She's haughty aquiline features to a tattered shape that shifted and moved as if caught in a non-existent breeze. "*Ay qei*," the shadow whispered. "It wants you. It wants what you have."

Ay qei was Khaitanese for the sort of lost soul that wandered the earth seeking justice, or at least vengeance. Chou wasn't equipped to handle them. He was a sorcerer, not a Priest. Fighting an urge to go looking for his mother, Chou said, "It's on the other side of that door?"

"It is," Simon said, sounding thoroughly and justifiably terrified. "I think it's trying to get through."

That was obvious. Chou could see the door move beneath the thing's touch, the metal bending and deforming then returning to normal, as if it were a sheet of silk pressed by a dancer's hands. The last time he'd seen anything remotely similar had been when they'd found those men flattened into another dimension. They'd only freed half and in some cases, half was all too literally true.

This wasn't the same. Chou could feel the energies flowing around him, the ghostly forces at the edges of his understanding. Remembering his lessons, he knew there was only one choice left. "Simon? We'd better run."

Flashlights flickering, barely showing the ground ahead of them, Chou and Simon rushed up the hallway. As he ran, Chou tried to think of damage control. The door had been twisting and tearing open just moments before and the ghost was right behind them. That, though, wasn't as worrisome as Simon seeing something he wasn't supposed to.

"What is this place?" Simon asked, gasping as they ran. "I didn't know there was anything like this under Strikersport."

"My grandfather put in a passage from his factory to the train station. Made it easier for his people to get their equipment back and forth." The hall was a good ten foot wide and equally tall. There was even a track in the middle that allowed small carts to be dragged along by equally small engines. When Chou and Robby had been kids, their grandfather had given them rides.

"That'd be Robert Joseph McLeod, right? The one you and your brother are named after?"

Chou agreed, amused despite the urgency of the situation. Even when chased by a hungry ghost intent on the Gods knew what, Simon insisted on gathering every fact he could about everything he saw. The trouble was, what would the would-be reporter do when he noticed certain details?

The question became moot a few minutes later as Chou spotted a strange faint glow ahead of him. Small but getting larger, there was something familiar about it that worried at him. They both skidded to a halt as the thing approached. "*Shi shi*?" Simon gasped. "What is it doing here. How is it here?"

Padding closer, the beast glared at Chou and Simon with an expression suggesting he was thoroughly and completely out of patience. It was the sort of look Chou's parents got when he and Robby caused trouble. "I don't suppose you'd let us pass?" The *shi shi* growled, the sound so like his mother when he'd forgotten his homework that Chou swallowed hard, half-expecting to be sent to his room. "I'm sorry. Whatever it is we've done to upset you, we can't stay here—"

The *shi shi* moved towards Chou threateningly and he reached into his pocket, intending to draw his weapon and found the cub instead. "Wait. Are you looking for this?" He held out transformed statue.

An angry growl turned to a roar of pure fury and Chou realized his trick—intended to conceal the sculpture from its would-be thieves—had worked too well. "No, don't be mad. It's all right. I didn't hurt it at all. Just let me—here. Like this." Never had he cast a transformation so quickly. Cold false ice shifted and he swayed, feeling the effort of too much magic too fast. "See?" He held out the cub as it squirmed in the palm of his hand, purple black eyes wide as it shook itself.

Immediately the lion leapt forward, snatching the cub in his paws. Simon's shadows moved, catching at him and he roared again in panic, nearly clawing Chou's cheek in his terror. "No!" Chou ordered. "Don't. He just wants his baby."

The shadows backed away and so did the lion, carrying his cub in his mouth. Chou was about to tell the lion not to be afraid, but then he felt the wave of negative energy coming from the other direction. "Uh oh," he muttered. "Not good."

Simon looked back, Ba She's shadows surrounding him as he stared. It wasn't one hungry ghost. Nor even a few. Dozens upon dozens, all shambling towards them, slowing, then speeding again. The lion set the cub down and moved to guard them all.

Drawing a scarf from his pocket, Chou set it waving. He was pushing his strength after all his other spell-work but he had to try. There were too many hungry ghosts to fight. Focusing his magic on the walls, he squeezed and twisted them together, tightening the metal shut around the ghosts.

If they'd been the kind of spirits bound to the world but not quite connected to it, they'd have walked straight through. This night, as the Festival drew closer, they had a physical presence that could be blocked. Not stopped, though. That would take more power than a small young sorcerer like Chou could manage.

"All of you, come on!" Chou called, picking up the lion cub again. "We have to run." The ghosts were stretching their arms through the cracks in the wall, pushing forward despite the way their bodies distorted. It wouldn't be long before they got through.

"I don't think we can outrun those things," Simon said, dashing after him, Ba She's shadows doing their best to force the ghosts back.

"I have a way," Chou countered as they rushed through the dark hallway, their path lit by the *shi shi* running alongside them. The creature could escape, Chou knew. He was faster than any ghost, even on this night. But he stayed close to protect his cub and for that Chou was profoundly grateful.

Leading Simon into grandfather McLeod's workshop, Chou paused to look at his companion. "I don't have a choice about letting you see this," he said. "But if one word of this gets out, I promise, I'll— I'll—I don't know what I'll do but you won't like it."

"Does it have to do with your mother being Dragon?" Simon asked and

" I DON'T BLAME THE SURVIVORS FOR BEING ANGRY... "

when Chou stared at him, added, "She does a pretty good job hiding it. I wouldn't have realized but for the way you reacted to her. Is Tiger your father?"

Chou blinked, staring in confusion. He'd been so busy trying to follow his mother's orders he'd not thought about the man wearing Tiger's mask. Conall McLeod didn't do a great deal of fighting, but Chou knew he could. Mudan had taught them all to protect themselves. "Might be," he admitted grumpily. "And this is wasting time."

"True," Simon agreed. "What are you planning? That metal dragon critter?"

Chou would have, but sensed Meng was busy elsewhere. "No. But there's *Yuan*." He went to the big garage door on the other side and tugged it up, revealing Tiger's big black motorcycle. Tiger wouldn't like him borrowing it but Chou didn't care. He climbed on and started the bike, setting her engine purring. "Get on behind me. And hold tight, because we're going straight to Chinatown."

"How is that a problem?" Simon asked, climbing on obediently. At the same time, the *shi shi* moved to join them and Chou was certain he could follow. "I already know the road is straight."

"Who said anything about roads?" Chou asked, kicking *Yuan* into gear and sending her flying out of the world and into the rift. He just hoped his grandfather was ready for company.

Chapter Eight
Tours of McLeod Motors Must be Requested in Advance

"I'm not sure he realizes I'm his niece."

"I did mention it. He ignored me. I think he's mistaken me for pure Japanese."

"Yes, father. Uncle Wugong is an idiot."

"And badly in need of glasses."

"And a thump to the head."

"Which I will provide should the opportunity present itself." Hoshi paused, adding, "And if he gives me reason."

"And I will be very careful not to let his centipedes bite me."

"You still haven't answered my question, father. Why would someone from Batsu be here in California? I thought they never leave their village except to trade."

"Yes, mother, I remember you asking me to keep an eye out for a *shi shi* cub statue. The only one I've seen was made of ceramic, though, not marble."

"I suppose someone could have transformed it. Or hidden its true appearance."

"Really? It came from their village? How many were there? And why is it important?"

"That's—not good. I don't blame the survivors for being angry, if that's the case. But why wait ten years?"

"None? At all? But how—?"

"I see. No wonder you're worried."

"Yes. I'll do my best. Aunt Mudan doesn't know. Should I tell her?"

"You're right, knowing her she's probably figured it out by now."

"And if she hasn't, I'll tell her everything you've told me."

"And I'll be careful, I promise."

Hanging up the phone, Hoshi Feng sighed. Getting hold of her parents required perfect timing, thanks to their being in Khaitan; nearly on the other side of the world. It was hard enough contacting people in that region. It was difficult and sometimes impossible to reach a magical land with a tenuous connection to the human world.

Yet it couldn't be helped. Her father, Zhanchi, had accepted a job as commander of Khaitan's small air force and her mother was now the Itinerant Magistrate of Khaitan's Western Quarter. Both would gladly help her with this problem, but even Khaitan's best flyer couldn't get to Strikersport in time. Besides, dragons would be far too noticeable.

Sitting down behind Conall McLeod's desk, Hoshi put the phone—specially designed to allow communication with Khaitan—back in its hidey-hole. The room was quiet, not because the workshop was empty or its workers on break, but because she'd switched on the soundproofing device Uncle Conall had installed for privacy. The window was darkened as well, preventing unwanted guests from looking through to see what the office's occupants were up to.

Switching off the soundproofing, Hoshi was surprised by shouts and pounding on the office door. "Oh, please. Don't tell me there's more trouble." She flipped another switch to see what was going on and sighed. "Lovely, just lovely. Talk about that silly devil and he shows up."

Feng Wugong was out there with several members of his gang, as well as the illusionist he'd been working with back in the temple. He had Uncle Conall's men rounded up in a corner, a dozen *jiangshi* bouncing in place around them. The hopping corpses weren't real, Hoshi knew, but the maintenance crew couldn't know that. And, ridiculous though they might seem to those who'd never seen them personally, no one wanted to be face to face with a hopping ghost.

While Hoshi could have escaped unnoticed, she knew from her father's stories that her uncle was capable of bull-headed obstinacy above and beyond the call of duty. 'You'd think my brother was born in the year of the ox instead of the dog', Zhanchi had said once. 'He's so insistent on being right he forgets to be correct.'

Opening the door and dodging sideways so her uncle's big fist didn't hit her nose, Hoshi eyed Wugong with annoyance. "Uncle, father's right. You really are a nuisance." She spoke in Cantonese, knowing her uncle hated the English language no matter how well he spoke it.

"How dare you call me uncle, you—"

Before he finished the sentence, Hoshi exerted her magic, creating an image between them of her father. "Because—as I tried to tell you before—you are my uncle. My father is Feng Zhanchi."

Wugong stared from the image to Hoshi, then back again. Half-expecting him to ignore her, despite her claim, she shifted the image's appearance to show her father when he was younger; a boyish air-jockey wearing the neat black uniform of the CNAC and a cocky grin. "Does this help?" she asked, trying to keep her patience.

"You're Zhanchi's girl? Him and that Fukushima woman's daughter? But the last time I saw you, you were this high." Wugong waved his hand towards his waist.

"I was five, Uncle Wugong. I've done some growing since." Hoshi was surprised it hadn't taken more talking to get the point across. "Now what do you want? If you're looking for Uncle Conall, he went down to Trendle Tower to help Aunt Mudan with something."

"It's that westerner woman I want. She's a sorceress—"

"She's a priestess of Meng Huang Hsiang, uncle. Not a mere sorceress. What do you want from her?" The sound of someone whimpering outside the office reminded Hoshi of the *jiangshi*. "And would you mind, terribly, letting those people out there go? They don't have anything to do with this."

"But I needed hostages to get that woman of McLeod's—"

"Mudan Chang. Daughter of the master of the Jeen Loon, Cheh Chang.

She doesn't belong to Uncle Conall and she isn't a white woman pretending to be Chinese."

"I never said she was white—" At Hoshi's raised brow, Wugong corrected himself sulkily. "All right, maybe I did once. I know she's Chang's daughter. But those Jeen Loon people aren't proper Chinese either. She's a westerner. An American. What am I supposed to call her?"

"You could try Mrs. McLeod, or possibly Mudan, if you're close enough to her," a voice said in English. "I mean, that's her name, after all."

Both Hoshi and Wugong looked towards the speaker and Hoshi sighed in relief, relaxing just a bit. She'd half-expected another one of the many gangs currently infesting Strikersport. The speaker being Officer Jarvis meant she didn't have to fight. Yet.

Wugong took a step towards Officer Jarvis. "You again. How did you find me?" This time he spoke in English, and Hoshi was startled to realize the policeman had understood their conversation earlier.

"I actually came to speak with Mr. McLeod." Officer Jarvis eyed Wugong cautiously, scanning the area around him. "No centipedes. Have you finally run out?"

Returning to Chinese, Wugong said, "Tell this ignorant white man I have no intention of answering."

Officer Jarvis started, blinked and said, "I—understood what you said. Oh dear. This is getting more complicated by the minute." He took off his hat and scratched his head, adding, "I don't think it extends to my speaking the language, though, or does it?"

"You are speaking English to my ears," Hoshi said. "Uncle?" Realizing Wugong had sulkily turned away, she added, "If he hears Chinese, I don't think he plans on confirming it."

Wugong's silence relaxed Officer Jarvis a little. Not so much that he wasn't paying attention, but he no longer looked as if he expected an attack any minute. "I can see that. I don't suppose Mr. McLeod is here?"

Once again, Hoshi explained, "Uncle Conall went to help Aunt Mudan with a problem at the hotel." One minute the man had been going over Hoshi's course work with her, the next he'd run off, responding to a chime from his pocket watch. Hoshi still didn't know why he'd gone, just that his wife needed his help. She wasn't sure how he knew, but it was obviously urgent.

Officer Jarvis frowned. "I'd better go find him."

"What do you want that foolish idiot for, anyway?" Wugong demanded suddenly. "He's useless."

"Remember the black stuff we ran into, over at the casino?"

"That hellfire? I know."

"Black stuff?" Hoshi repeated, a sneaking suspicion worrying at her. "What sort of black stuff?"

After a moment of hesitation, Officer Jarvis asked, "I got the impression Mr. McLeod is teaching you engineering?"

"He's helping me with my degree, yes."

"And you're a sorcerer?"

"I am. What does that have to do with anything."

"Did Mr. McLeod tell you about last year's incident?"

Hoshi agreed, adding, "I'm not allowed to work with rift engineering alone, yet. If you're looking for someone who can help with that sort of thing, Robby's probably a better choice."

An odd look crossed Officer Jarvis' face, a smirk Hoshi didn't understand at all. "I don't need any for myself, really. But I'm afraid someone else may be fiddling with it. I'm pretty sure that's what that stuff that grabbed you was, Wuko—I'm sorry, Wugong. My pronunciation isn't good and I know you're not the Monkey King."

Wugong sniffed. "Why anyone would want to be, including him, is the question. And I don't care what name you give that stuff, it's hellfire, plain and simple."

"I don't know about plain and simple," Officer Jarvis countered. "I do know the last time someone opened up a rift around here, we nearly had a whole house implode. I'd like to avoid it happening again."

"Why should I care? The only thing that matters to us is dealing with that fool Andersen and his women. They ran off before we could catch up."

Wugong's partner turned from her illusion, which at least made the hopping ghosts stop hopping. "Those ones. Those lying ones. I told you, Wugong. You should not have helped them."

"We need them to trust us, to not realize your purpose, Yahgmar. It was a risk we had to take. They're fools, but even fools may realize the truth when it stares them in the face."

Hoshi didn't point out the irony of her uncle's words, saying instead, "Madam, would you release Uncle Conall's crew? It would make our discussion easier. Besides, I'm sure you're growing tired, after all the magic you've had to wield today."

The woman stared at Hoshi blankly. Then, with unexpected effort, she raised a hand and dismissed her spell. Hoshi frowned, as a sorcerer herself, she knew ending a spell should be no more difficult than setting a heavy weight down. She eyed the woman, sensing wrongness but at a loss as to why.

The pit-crew looked at Hoshi. "Miss Feng? Will you be all right?" Carlos asked bravely, his face damp with sweat and his hands shaking. She didn't blame him in the slightest, given what they'd seemed to be faced with.

"I can handle the situation, Carlos. You needn't worry about me. Uncle Wugong is not a good man, but he knows what his brother will do to him if he causes me harm."

Wugong huffed. "As if I attack family out of hand."

"Do you wish to say so to my father?" Seeing he had no answer, Hoshi continued, "Go home, all of you. And stay safe."

Granted release, the pit-crew ran off, the littlest, Sissy Jones, looking back a few times as if she yearned to stay and help. Only Hoshi's gesture made her move on.

Turning back to the woman called Yahgmar, Hoshi said, "Thank you, ma'am."

Yahgmar's answer came in slow, polite, Batsu. Not knowing the language, Hoshi bowed a little, saying, "Forgive me, but I don't understand."

"I did," Officer Jarvis said, sounding unnerved and proving he truly was understanding languages he had no way of knowing. "She said, 'I am not here to bully weaklings like those. I am here to punish the guilty.' Like that fellow who attacked Mr. Andersen back in the casino. Mr. Rogers. Is he an ally of yours?"

To Hoshi's relief, Yahgmar answered in Cantonese this time, "I do not know him."

Wugong snorted. "He's Andersen's tool. Not a very good one at that. He didn't even notice us taking Andersen into the temple basement this morning."

Ignoring Wugong's complaint, Officer Jarvis asked, "Madam, could you explain what justice you're looking for? I get the impression Mr. Andersen, or someone from his company, perhaps, did something to anger you? I can't promise anything under American law; I don't know what he's done. But I promise to try and help resolve your argument with him."

Yahgmar turned slowly to look at Officer Jarvis and Hoshi swallowed. Being an illusionist, she should have noticed before, but now she looked more carefully, she realized the woman was concealed beneath a veil of normalcy. Knowing it was there and trained to look beyond such things, she couldn't help doing so. What she saw was enough to make her gag. The woman was a walking corpse.

"What is it, Hoshi?"

Seeing a pleading look in the dead woman's empty eyes, Hoshi said, "Nothing, Officer Jarvis. Ma'am, you were about explain why you're here?" Hoshi already knew from her mother, but this was Yahgmar's story to tell.

The tale wasn't a pleasant one. Batsu village was a small place that existed partly in the real world and partly in Khaitan. Subsisting on trade goods; carvings and wrought work, they'd developed forms of magic involving illusion and transformation. A private and insular people, they'd had little contact with either world.

All would have remained the same if outsiders hadn't come to the village after the war. An American geologist working for Andersen Mining Corporation had become lost in the Taklamakan desert. Saved by one of the village's traders, they'd been brought taken in and helped.

While recovering, the geologist had slipped away from his keepers and discovered a pair of *shi shi* statues guarding the village's greatest treasure: twin void stones—*daitsushi*—that permitted the village to exist both within and outside of Khaitan. The geologist had realized the ball and the cub both radiated an energy similar to the sort he'd been looking for. He'd tried to buy them from the village headwoman, but had been refused.

Mentioning the statues made Officer Jarvis frown thoughtfully. "Was the *shi shi* at my Aunt Harriet's one of the pair?" At Yahgmar's agreement, he asked, "Are they known for coming to life?"

"When called properly, yes," Yahgmar acknowledged. "But only one of us had that talent; Ma the Horse, my husband. He was the first killed when the geologist brought mercenaries to our village to help him steal the *daitsushi*. They broke the female *shi shi*, trying to get her cub. As for the male, they took him and his jewel intact."

"He didn't have it when I saw him," Officer Jarvis noted.

"It was removed before the statue was sold to the Jeen Loon."

"I—see." Officer Jarvis gestured apologetically, adding, "I interrupted. I presume you tried to stop the mercenaries and some of your people were killed?"

The effort to speak obviously exhausted Yahgmar. "They murdered us all. They slaughtered us. They stole our sacred treasures, and they left our village burning. I was the last, dying on the altar of our Gods, with only hatred and vengeance to serve me." Yahgmar allowed her illusion to fade, revealing her true appearance and Officer Jarvis stared, wide-eyed. "It took years to gain enough power, but my people have been granted life with which to seek our killers."

Slowly, Officer Jarvis asked, "Like that Mr. Rogers fellow?"

Rogers was the man who'd been with Mrs. Andersen, the one wearing the brooch Hoshi remembered her mother describing. There'd been something off about him, even then.

"I do not know his name. But if he carried one of our treasures, he carried our vengeance with it. The guilty ones must and will pay. Both the stranger and his women."

"I don't understand. Carried your treasure? Carried your vengeance?"

It hit Hoshi what Yahgmar meant. "She's saying that the souls of the dead are inside the stolen treasures. So anyone who wears them is possessed." She reached out, cautiously touching Yahgmar's dry and desiccated hand. "But your vengeance is hurting people who had nothing to do with your village's death. This can't go on."

"I must have my vengeance." The answer didn't surprise Hoshi. Ghosts like Yahgmar were almost impossible to dissuade. Their only care was their cause and nothing would turn them from it but its completion or their destruction.

"An understandable desire," Officer Jarvis said gently. "But right now, we have another, bigger problem. I've been told the timing of all this means there's some sort of—path—being created between our world and Khaitan. Is this something you want? Because it's not just your enemies who'll suffer. If I understand what I've been told, the Feast of Hungry Ghosts is coming, and I don't think Strikersport can handle it."

It was Wugong who shrugged. "We're supposed to worry about westerners? It was a westerner caused the trouble in the first place."

Annoyed, because she was, herself, an American citizen despite everything, Hoshi said, "One westerner is guilty. Must thousands pay for one criminal's fault?" At Yahgmar's glare, she added, "It won't just be the people of Strikersport who'll be in danger. Khaitan's affected as well. Do you think that's a good thing?"

"I—do not," the woman admitted. "Khaitan is where it is, and as it is, for a reason. Upsetting the balance would cause far more damage than I ever desired. But I must find the man who did this to us. I must make him pay for what he has done. Him and the one he worked for."

"As I've said, I'm not sure American law can help you." Officer Jarvis spread his hands helplessly. "But I do promise to help you find him and to try and stop whatever he and the others are up to. I've a bad feeling Horne has access to rift technology now, and I'd prefer it if Strikersport didn't wind up falling straight into the void."

Hoshi agreed. "I, too, have certain philosophical objections to such an event."

Since Officer Jarvis had dismissed his taxi they took Hoshi's car into town. An elegant lavender vehicle over twenty years old, it'd been the beloved toy of a good friend of her father's. He'd gifted it to Hoshi when she'd visited Khaitan a year back, claiming the car was bored. Hoshi didn't doubt him. Shen Lunghua's duties kept him too busy to drive these days.

Sitting beside Hoshi, Officer Jarvis ignored Wugong's mutterings in the back. It was obvious her uncle was almost powerless without his centipedes. Likely, Wugong kept a few back for emergencies, but he'd used his magic with such profligate enthusiasm Hoshi doubted there were many left.

Using the brief respite to explain what he knew to Hoshi, Officer Jarvis ended with, "I sent my men to take the prisoners to jail. Officer Kenneth and my cousin have gone to see Mr. Chang, to see if he knows anything about Mr. Andersen."

"I see. And the *shi shi*?"

"He went to look for his cub. Robby took it with him."

That amused Hoshi. "He would. He likes lions."

Changing the subject, Officer Jarvis asked, "Robby told me your father is Mr. McLeod's business partner?"

"That's right. He and Mr. McLeod met in Shanghai in the '30s," Hoshi explained. "They became friends and Mr. Chang hired them both for Jeen Loon airlines. Father's in Khaitan, now, though. The Queen asked him to command her Air Force."

Officer Jarvis stared at her. "Air Force? Khaitan has an Air Force?"

"Well, yes. Why wouldn't they?" The man's mouth worked as he tried to wrap his mind around the idea and Hoshi took pity on him. "It's a magical kingdom, and technology doesn't work well there, but most of Khaitan's Air Force are dragons or other flying beings. Besides, just because a place is magical doesn't mean it's backward. Khaitan isn't Disney, after all."

That set Officer Jarvis laughing. "I suppose not." He was about to ask more, but they were just entering downtown Strikersport and the sudden wail of police sirens interrupted him. "The devil?"

"What is it? What is that noise? It is terrible," Yahgmar said, leaning forward. "Why do I feel so cold?"

An animated corpse ought not feel anything, much less a chill, and Hoshi realized she felt it as well. So did Officer Jarvis. "The rift again?" he asked, opening his window so he could see out. "Uhm—Miss Yahgmar, I thought you said those treasures of yours possessed people. Do they also turn them to *jiangshi*?"

While Hoshi wondered how he'd known the name for the monsters, Yahgmar tried to look out the window too. Only when Wugong switched places with her did she see what Officer Jarvis was looking at. She hissed through her teeth, "Those of us allowed this non-life have no such magic." There was a faint note of doubt in her voice, as if she suspected something. If so, she didn't admit to it.

Slowing her car to a halt, and backing up a little so she, too, could see down the alley to the next street, Hoshi stared. At first glance, the crowd of tattered, ragged, stumbling men and women might be mistaken for homeless drunks, banded together in a mob and stumbling towards the center of town. But closer examination showed desiccated limbs, jagged teeth and a notable inability to actually walk. They weren't dressed the way most *jiangshi* were, but then she doubted the Batsu had been granted proper burial.

"Don't look at me for help with those things," Wugong said grimly. "I can fight humans, even without my centipedes. But *jiangshi* are right out of my area of expertise."

"And mine," Yahgmar added. "There was only one of us with the knowledge and she is gone—" She fell silent, refusing to share her thoughts.

Grimly, Officer Jarvis said, "We'd better get inside, then."

Trendle Tower was surrounded by police when Hoshi parked on a nearby street. "Why so far away?" Wugong demanded, jerking his thumb at Officer Jarvis. "He can get us through. Those police do what he says."

"I have no doubt he can and will, Uncle." Hoshi got her backpack out of the trunk. "But this is Shen Lunghua's beloved Yancai. Would you care to explain to him how she came to be damaged, should whatever is wrong inside the tower find its way outside?"

That silenced Wugong, allowing Officer Jarvis to ask, "What's in there?" He indicated the backpack Hoshi slung over her shoulder.

"My equipment. Given what you said about the rift device, it may come in handy." There was more to it than that, but she didn't want to explain unless she had to. "We'd better hurry. Before those *jiangshi* make things worse."

They hurried down the street and past the police cars surrounding the building. Police had been arresting thugs left and right, but the sudden appearance of the *jiangshi* had been enough to send everyone—criminal and law alike—scurrying for cover. The *jiangshi* themselves were breaking through the big glass doors, ignoring everything and everyone in their path in their desperate need to get inside.

"They are—I know them." Yahgmar's voice cracked with emotion. "Taga? Dourig? This can't be. They can't be here. I buried them. I buried them all!"

The *jiangshi* didn't respond to the woman's voice. Of course, if Hoshi remembered her folklore correctly, they wouldn't. *Jiangshi* were mindless corpses, walking only because their spirits—or *po* souls—had failed to leave their bodies when they'd died. They acted only on instinct, craving living human energy to fill the gaping void their *hun* souls had left.

The glass shattered enough to let the broken, ragged, bodies through. Hoshi supposed Yahgmar hadn't the wherewithal to give the poor things a proper burial. Hopefully that could be rectified when this mess was over. Given there was anyone left to do so.

Somewhere inside the building, someone shrieked, "Where is my *fu* dog! My *fu* dog is gone! Why did my *fu* dog melt?" Distorted by rage, it was almost unrecognizable, but Hoshi knew it had to be Mrs. Andersen. Her husband's voice came after, telling the woman to stop fussing over unimportant details when he had plans to make.

Cautiously, ignoring Officer Jarvis' attempt to stop her, Hoshi moved forward and hid inside the doorway. The room beyond was a mess, decorations scattered all over the place, signs of a truly impressive fight. No bodies, but the police might have dealt with them before the *jiangshi* showed up.

Those same *jiangshi* were crowded in the lobby, hopping in place patiently, as if waiting their turn with the clerk. Their presence was a wrongness in the world, not just because they were there at all, but because they weren't attempting to rip the sole human occupants of the room to shreds.

Peering around the corner, Hoshi spotted Mrs. Andersen and her companion at the second floor balcony. Mrs. Andersen looked furious, her pretty clothes soaking wet and stained with blotches of pink and green. Her companion, Minerva, had the same long-suffering expression she'd had back at the *Jeen Loon.*

"*Shi shi,* Athena. It's a *shi shi.*"

"Yes. Right. *Shi shi.* Where is my *shi shi*?"

Another voice interrupted as an older man in a badly torn suit grabbed hold of Mrs. Andersen, snapping, "I don't care what you call it, woman. Stop making a drama of yourself."

Behind Hoshi, Officer Jarvis muttered, "She seems to make that mistake all the time. I wonder why?"

"Because she's a purblind idiot who can't be corrected?" Wugong demanded.

They all, even Yahgmar, looked at Wugong and it was Hoshi who asked, "You do know what you just said, don't you, Uncle?"

Crankily, Wugong muttered something Hoshi's father would not want her to know how to say. "I may be as bad, but I don't repeat myself every damned time—" Anxiously, he added, "Do I?"

"You do, a bit," Yahgmar assured him. "But—you don't go back to something once you do correct yourself. Mostly." Mrs. Andersen was, once more, using the wrong word and once more being corrected. Meanwhile, the *jiangshi* continued to roam around aimlessly.

Puzzled by the monsters' behavior, Hoshi asked Yahgmar, "Do you know why they're just standing there?"

"I—they have to have been summoned." Again there was a puzzled, worried, expression on Yahgmar's desiccated features, suggesting she suspected more than she admitted.

Meanwhile, Minerva was saying, "Don't worry, Athena. I've sent others to find the little one. Horne is more important."

"I was promised that *fu* cub. You promised me the *fu* cub."

At the same time Andersen grumbled. "I don't know why we should worry about that man. If he's fool enough to throw away the fortune he earned from me to be a common criminal, he's too foolish to concern ourselves with."

"*Shi shi,*" Minerva told Mrs. Andersen with the barely concealed impatience. "And Horne was always our target—sir. Remember?"

"Oh, yes. Of course."

Hoshi was about suggest they try sneaking into the building when a faint, familiar, sound drew her attention. "*Yuan?*" she muttered. The noise was a kind of thrumming flutter that seemed to work its way straight into the middle of her brain. Rift technology always had that effect on her.

Blackness shimmered towards the center of the room, a heaving, squirming, purple black sphere from which half a dozen men tumbled. One was twice the size of the others, an ogre formed of chaos, with a strangely human face. He held a device in his hand that glimmered with rift energies.

Officer Jarvis stared at the ogre. "Horne and his toy again. What the hell's happened to him?"

At the same time, three voices practically shrieked the gangster boss's name. Two came as no surprise, Mr. Andersen and Minerva. But the last drew everyone's attention as Yahgmar rushed out screaming, "I'LL KILL YOU!"

"Do I know you?" Horne mocked, purple smoke trailing out of his mouth as he spoke. "Oh, you look a bit familiar, if a little dry. Yahgmar, wasn't it? I thought I killed you." He raised the device and aimed it at the woman, its energies sinking her into the floor in a terrifyingly familiar way, until she was embedded in the solid surface, squirming around within the confines of the polished oak. "Always time to rectify that mistake."

"The same as last year. Again." Officer Jarvis sounded like he was trying not to be sick and Hoshi couldn't blame him. She hadn't been in Strikersport when The Voice and his minions had caused so much trouble, but she didn't need to be. Robby and Chou had waxed eloquent on the subject of the evil mastermind whose science had allowed him to thrust human flesh into solid matter.

"Last year?" Wugong demanded. "This happens all the time?"

Before Hoshi could even try to explain, the blackness from which Horne and his men had fallen began pulsing and shifting, bits and pieces of it stretching out and sucking in *jiangshi*. At the same time, strange, ragged, and translucent figures tore their way through the floor, rising from the abandoned station below.

"*Ay qei*?" Hoshi breathed, watching the ghostly forms envelop the *jiangshi*.

"*Ay qei*? Hungry ghosts? Like from the festival?"

"Yes. But I've never heard of them being so solid before." This was a disaster. All the magic and energies flowing through Strikersport had finally found an outlet. "We have to do something before things get worse."

"Such as?" Wugong demanded. "You are a mere illusionist, niece. This westerner's only advantage is his tie to the Black Eagle. And I am almost out of centipedes."

Swinging her backpack onto the floor, Hoshi told the two men, "I have a device to assist us, but I'll need time to set it up. Can you two keep me from being interrupted?"

Wugong and Officer Jarvis eyed each other mistrustfully. "Just stay out of my way, Westerner," Wugong grumbled. Then they took up a position between Hoshi and the fight.

The first order of business was keeping the rift from getting any larger. Horne wasn't helping. His device seemed to use rift energy to function. Every time he activated it the rift got a bit bigger and a bit more ragged. He didn't seem to notice the danger, or if he did, he didn't care. *Jiangshi* after *jiangshi* sank into the floor to join Yahgmar.

Nor did Horne notice that his enemies were hardly fazed at all by what he'd done to them. Human minds would be confused and disoriented, unable to do much more than flail wildly within the confines of the material they'd been embedded within. *Jiangshi* had no minds to befuddle and no sense of pain to stop them from fighting their way out of their prison. As for the *ay qei*, the device had no effect on them at all.

The only ones in danger from Horne's attack were the humans. The Andersens, Minerva, Wugong, Hoshi and Officer Jarvis, as well as the score of thugs who were obviously Andersen's employees. Fortunately for Hoshi's guards, Horne focused his attention on his would-be rival. Aside from the occasional stray gangster and *jiangshi*, neither Wugong, nor Officer Jarvis, were in danger. Yet.

Hoshi pulled her device from her backpack and slid her hand into the grip. A large cylinder ending in an elegant set of prongs, it was the result of months of research. Uncle Conall had been teaching her and Robby about rift energies and how to both use and negate them. They'd been working on a device similar to the one in Tiger's motorcycle, one that used a riftstone—a synthesized version of a *daitsushi*—to bind rift energies rather than fuel a machine.

The device Hoshi held was bulky and unaesthetic, but it was solid, and she was almost sure the design would work. The question was, could it operate on all this wild rift energy, rather than the riftstone she wasn't permitted to use yet? Moreover, could it handle the raw power surrounding them? The only thing to do was try.

Switching the device on, Hoshi set the controls to draw on the ambient

"TIGER, IS THERE ANYTHING MORE WE CAN DO?"

energies in the room. Magic and rift energies were as like to each other as a candle was to the sun. If the transducer Tiger had devised to keep his motorcycle's riftstone from overloading was insufficient, the thing would explode in her hands.

It shuddered, vibrating at such speed Hoshi felt as if she'd melt straight into the floor like Horne's victims. Forcing herself to focus, she drew on her magic, carefully building a shape in her mind. She'd learned it from a physics student in England, a pattern certain sorcerers used to contain magic and bind it to their will. She wasn't that sort of sorcerer, but with her device augmenting her illusions and giving them reality, she hoped it'd be enough.

The pattern shifted and she lost track of it. Shapes like this didn't occur in nature and she wasn't accustomed to them. Then her mathematics came to the rescue, as she intertwined her friend's quasicrystal lattice with a tesseract. Three dimensional space couldn't hold such a thing ordinarily, but with the rift energies behind it, a star formed around the tear. It shone brilliantly, its complex form seeming to twist in on itself as one watched.

"Oh, well done, youngster." The voice came from beside Hoshi and caused both Wugong and Officer Jarvis to turn and simultaneously kick and punch at what appeared to be thin air. "Hey! No need for violence. It's just me."

The air shimmered and a black clad figure—Tiger of the Golden Dragons—appeared. His black hat had been knocked askew, revealing a loose mane of jet black hair and a face hidden behind a painted on mask.

"You! Going to pretend you don't know me again?" Wugong demanded, aiming another kick Tiger's way. "You bastard!"

"Now, now, Wugong. Can't we let bygones be bygones?" Tiger asked. "Officer Jarvis, behind you." His warning was well-timed, because now that the rift was gone, all the *jiangshi* were once more free to attack. Fortunately, the monsters were among the weakest of their kind, easily knocked backwards by a well-aimed punch.

"Why didn't you show up earlier? We could have used the help."

"I've been busy up in the banquet hall, Wugong. We heard the commotion but had too many others to deal with. The vast majority of whom being Centipedes, by the way. Sorry about that. You really do need to hire a better class of crook."

Before her uncle could lose his temper, Hoshi asked, "Tiger, is there anything more we can do?" She clutched her device, all too aware of what would happen if what it contained broke free.

"That thing of yours needs to be gotten clear of the building. The higher the better. Can I take it now?"

Hoshi handed it to the man. "Just don't let anyone switch it off. You won't be able to reset it."

"Good. I'll get it to the roof before anything worse happens. Officer Jarvis? Wugong, would you two mind terribly accompanying me? I don't think our friends over there will cooperate and I could do with backup."

That made Hoshi glare at the man. "What about me?" He'd better not be telling her to go hide like a frightened child.

"You've another job, youngster. We're going to need help from the others to avoid an implosion." Tiger pointed east, towards Strikers Peak. "Get up to Chinatown, as fast as ever you can, and get help. You'll know who we need as soon as you get there, Dragon says."

Before Hoshi could open her mouth to ask another question, Tiger headed into the lobby, twisting and turning to evade the fight. After a brief look at each other, Wugong and Officer Jarvis followed behind.

Hoshi thought about rebelling but knew Dragon would have unkind words to say if she failed to get the help she'd been sent to retrieve. Unwillingly, she hurried outside and back to her car. She just hoped Cheh Chang was ready for company.

Chapter Nine
Strikersport is an excellent starting point for International Travel

Cheh Chang's house was likely getting quite full, Dragon mused. She was still in the banquet hall, waiting for her moment to act and listening to her God's voice as he showed her the events of the day. The children had all done well, but it was high time for the adults to take a hand. It'd been quite a display, she reflected. Rather like one of those silly 'B' movies the boys were so fond of. "Empire of the Eastern Star" perhaps?

"So they've all dumped themselves on the Old Man," she murmured. "I do hope he hadn't planned anything special tonight."

Three men ran past the banquet hall doors. Tiger, Officer Jarvis and that nuisance Feng Wugong. If Dragon didn't already know the Centipede gang's boss was—nominally—on their side she would have been concerned. The man had mellowed significantly from the vicious crook he'd been back in the day, but he was still untrustworthy and given to bouts of self-righteous stupidity.

A half-dozen men rushed after Tiger, their bodies flickering in and out as they tried to stay close to the rift. Their master was behind them, urging them on furiously, his body still swollen with the energies he'd absorbed. She'd feel sorry for the poor souls, embedded in Chaos as they were, if not for what they'd been trying to do. Rifts were dangerous things, tears in reality that could turn everything inside out, and those idiots had been playing with the power their technology had accessed as if it were a toy.

Thank the Gods Hoshi had sealed the rift Horne had created, if temporarily. Tiger could create controlled paths through the rift, but tears were beyond him. It'd taken an impressive combination of sorcery and technology for young Hoshi to contain the thing. Dragon would have to remember to tell Hikaru how well her daughter had done.

Thinking of Hikaru reminded Dragon of the reason for all this nonsense. The slaughter of Batsu village required redress neither Khaitanese nor American law could readily cope with. Yet their God demanded justice from his province's magistrate, despite the complications created by the lack of political ties between America and a land few realized existed.

Things were quieting outside the banquet hall and Dragon climbed down from the table to pick her way amongst the groaning forms of the thugs who'd attacked her for things she no longer had. She evaded a grasping hand from one of Wugong's men, leaning down and telling him in Chinese, "You should be grateful and rest. Things will just get worse from here and the less you are involved, the better."

Then she went to find the woman, Yahgmar, wasn't it? Perhaps, between the two of them, they could resolve this madness before someone brought the entirety of a magical kingdom into California. Dragon liked Khaitan, but not that much.

"Don't play with the damned thing!"

Tiger examined Hoshi's device, delighted by the brilliant pattern of lines forming an impossible shape. Really, she'd turned out to be quite the talent. Robby had the advantage of growing up around his father's equipment and being exposed to science of a sort most people never even heard of. Khaitan, on the other hand, relied on magic more, making Hoshi's ready comprehension that much more impressive.

"Did you hear what I said?" Wugong demanded sharply.

"It's fascinating. Don't you think it's fascinating?" Tiger spoke in Cantonese automatically, knowing Wugong hated speaking English. "Your niece does fine work, you know. You should be proud of her."

Wugong sneered. "She's smart, but she's just a girl. And why the hell are we even talking about this when we have the hordes of hell on our tails?"

"They're not all hordes of hell. Some of them are human. I—think?" William countered, and Tiger gave him a startled look. The young policeman had spoken in English but he'd obviously understood every word Tiger and Wugong had just said. When had William learned Cantonese? One picked up all sorts of languages in Strikersport, but the Chinese population used Mandarin almost exclusively, it being the closest dialect to Khaitan's main tongue.

When Tiger remarked on William's odd new skill, the younger man flushed. "One of those Immortals did it." He dodged sideways, kicking a *jiangshi* in the chin and sending it flying into the one behind it. "You—you do know about them, right?"

One of the things Tiger appreciated about William Jarvis was the care he took not to make assumptions about people. It was a rare attribute and one Tiger thought would get the young man far. "I know. Dragon kept me appraised all day." He tapped his earphone, with the small device he'd built to let him and his partner communicate around town.

They ran up the stairs, barely evading the *ay qei* tearing through the nearest wall. Fortunately, the vengeful spirits weren't interested in them. The Bear Gulch gang and the others—the ones from Boston—had their complete and undivided attention. "Ever feel ignored?"

"You know, I was just wondering the same thing. The only reason they're here is because Horne and his men are after us." William glanced back over his shoulder, forcing Wugong to catch him when he stumbled. "Sorry."

"We know what's behind us. There's no need to look." Wugong was actually scared, but given Horne, or what had been Horne, wanted to rip the three of them to shreds, Tiger couldn't blame him. "Why does he even care about that thing?"

"I think it's the source of his strength." Tiger had watched the fight from the other side of the room and seen how Horne had kept growing every time he used his phasing device. That thing would have to be dealt with, but without a power source, it was useless. Horne, on the other hand, was a different story. He might not have the rift increasing his strength, but he'd absorbed quite enough already.

Someone shrieked ahead of them, the sound growing closer as they ran. "GIVE ME MY *FU* DOG!" Another voice corrected the speaker, but to little avail. It seemed Mrs. Andersen was incapable of being corrected. Rather like certain other people Tiger knew.

As if on cue, Wugong muttered, "Does that woman ever learn?" Tiger eyed his old enemy turned ally and something of his expression must have been visible even with his mask. "I know, I know. But even I can change my mind sometimes."

Tiger considered that. "It's such a rare thing I'm hard put to respond." He ducked as Wugong swung at him. The strike was half-hearted, intended to remind Tiger that they weren't friends and never would be. They were, however, allies, and Tiger didn't retaliate. Instead, he grabbed Wugong's wrist and pulled him sideways just before a clawed hand reached out for him.

The owner of the hand wore an expensive dress, the same one Mrs. Andersen had sported earlier. If it was the same, its wearer had transformed and enlarged: Matted hair, torn out in chunks from a scalp that looked more like a skull; Teeth that hadn't seen a dentist ever; Diseased skin that might slough off any moment; Jagged fingernails half torn from their place. Oh, yes, and a terminal case of body odor that reminded Tiger of an abattoir.

"GIVE ME MY *FU* DOG!" The demand was accompanied by another swipe. For the thousandth time her companion, Minerva, repeated, "*Shi shi!* You ignorant hag. How many times do I have to tell you that?"

Tiger told the monster, "We don't have a *fu* dog. Or a *shi shi*, for that matter. You might try downstairs and to your left." Then he sprinted past the pair, headed for another set of stairs. They didn't have time for questions. Not when the rift might break free again any minute.

He just hoped he could get to the roof first.

The lobby was empty of three dimensional bodies, but its floor was a different story. Dragon reflected that Miss Trendle wouldn't be happy if they had to take the whole thing up, the way Conall McLeod had had to remove a wall from the newspaper's offices a year earlier. Especially given it'd be for the same reason.

Most of those embedded in the floor—or rather in the half-step sideways dimension they actually inhabited—were *jiangshi*. Badly twisted bodies, partially decomposed, the scars of their death was still visible in their flesh. Each and every one had a bullet hole in the middle of their foreheads. When Dragon saw the five year old child amongst the bodies, she ground her teeth. She'd been told what had happened to the Batsu, but seeing it made the whole thing personal. Unnecessarily so. One of her own—Tsui—had fallen in this fight as well.

Something dragged itself out of the floor ahead of Dragon and she waited for the spirit to break free of its prison. Yahgmar had to leave her decayed flesh behind to escape, but she was too stubborn to remain trapped for long. She stared around furiously, spotting the *jiangshi* struggling free around her. "Who brought them here? Who dared?"

"I don't have an answer to that question," Dragon said, causing the woman to spin her head—and only her head—to look at her. "Am I addressing Headwoman Yahgmar of the Batsu?"

Yahgmar agreed. "You're that woman Wugong goes on about. Dragon, among other things."

"We need not discuss what else Wugong calls me, Headwoman. Suffice it to say I am here to put a stop to this nonsense."

Before Dragon could say another word, Yahgmar rushed her, a bodiless spirit attempting to possess the closest person. Dragon didn't bother trying to evade, allowing her God's power to flow through her, the heat of his fever dizzying. Yahgmar screamed, thrown back by the force of Meng Huang Hsiang's energy and Dragon said, "I am the Dreamlord's priestess, Headwoman. He suffers none but himself to use me as a vessel."

Staring, the vengeful spirit whispered, "But how?"

"My people have ties to Khaitan. That is enough explanation for now." Dragon examined Yahgmar critically. The poor thing had been through enough. It was time and past to set her and her kin to rest. "Come with me. I will be needing your help all too soon."

Though obviously unwilling to cooperate, Yahgmar came to a decision quickly. "Very well. But this had best not be a betrayal. Wugong warned me you were dangerous and not to be trusted."

"Wugong sees himself in others." Dragon led the way to the other side of the room. "Nor is he the most intelligent of men. Else he would have approached this nonsense differently." She pushed the elevator button and was relieved when the doors opened. With all the magic and rift power running rampant, she hadn't been sure a simple machine would still work.

"Is it wise to trust machinery at such a time?"

"Speed is essential, Headwoman. And I must save my strength for what comes." Dragon stepped aboard the elevator and once Yahgmar joined her, hit the top button. "In the meantime, lacking anything else to do, you might tell me who among your people has the power to summon *jiangshi* and *ay qei*."

Evasively, Yahgmar asked, "Why would you think that any of us did?"

"You are an illusionist. The one who used the *shi shi* cub to command its father was a giver of life to the inanimate. Neither sorcery can call forth monsters such as *jiangshi* or *ay qei*."

"So? It's almost the Feast of Hungry Ghosts. How do you know one of my kin had anything to do with those poor dead souls?"

"The *jiangshi* trapped within the floor are your people's corpses. Their spirits the *ay qei*. Will you still tell me they have nothing to do with this nonsense? Do you wish to say they came here on their own power, so very far from home, at such a convenient time?"

Yahgmar wilted. "No. I didn't want to admit it, but—my daughter, Taranga. She learned to command monsters, to control them and bind them to her will. But for her to use our people so? That's more than I want to accept."

"I am a mother as well," Dragon said quietly. "Our children do not always follow our desires. But I think Taranga acts out of love and loss. Understandably so, even if it has brought more trouble than this city ever asked for, or requires."

The door opened onto the roof, where Tiger, Officer Jarvis and Wugong were holding off a group of men whose bodies pulsed with rift energy. Horne was struggling with the hag, the creature growing as it drew on his life force. Meanwhile, Andersen's men were trying to protect their boss, while the *ay qei* swiped at any who stood still long enough to be touched.

The sound of a motorcycle filled the air, louder than the shouts and howls of those on the roof and Dragon looked up to see Robby circling around the building on a jet black bike, Stephanie Frazer clinging to him. The quicksilver dragon, Meng, came next, howling in answer as he carried Chou and Simon Lee around the rooftop.

A third sound—a high pitched buzzing—drew Dragon's attention.

Hoshi, bringing the toy helicopter she and Robby had built in for a landing. A moment later a pillar of smoke formed in the middle of the fight, the rumble and hiss of the hottest fire burning at its center; Gilly, arriving in his own, inimitable, fashion; accompanied by the male *shi shi* and Rosamund as well.

"And, it seems, we'll have help. Which is good," Dragon said quietly. "As I believe we will need it."

Tiger dodged Horne's grasping claw. "Give that back!" the gang boss growled, trying to snatch Hoshi's device away.

"Oh, I don't think I will," Tiger told the transformed man. "You're quite large enough already. No need to be greedy."

A serpent formed of smoke and fire forced its way between several of Horne's men and William, a *shi shi* at its side. To Tiger's surprise, Rosamund Krane was sitting sidesaddle on the lion's neck. She patted it gently, ignoring everyone's stares. "Billy, we're here to help. What would you like us to do?"

"I'd have preferred you stay out of this. Not bring a whole circus into the fight," William grumbled.

"We didn't bring the whole circus. Mr. Rogers and Boopsie are still back with Mr. Cheh, you know."

"Thank God for small favors." William turned his attention on Gilly. "Is there anything you can do about that thing Tiger's got by the tail?"

Gilly turned his huge head so he could eye the rift Hoshi's device contained. "Oh no, boss man. That's out of my league. I managed that one itty bitty rip last time but that thing's out of my bailiwick."

The news was unsurprising and Tiger was about to say as much when the hag who'd been Mrs. Andersen and her 'sister' Minerva flung themselves at him. "Give me back my *fu* dog!" the hag screeched.

"I don't have a *fu* dog, or a *shi shi* for that matter." Tiger suspected they wanted the cub currently zipped up in Robby's jacket, cuddled against the boy like a pet puppy. He didn't know the pair's intent, but he had no intention of letting them realize where it was. He swung the contained rift away from Horne at the same time, to the gang boss's bellowed fury.

"All of you come to me," Dragon called suddenly and while it was easier said than done, Tiger dodged, firing off his weapon as he shifted and twisted his way between the enemy. William and Wugong followed behind, with Gilly simply rising above the crowd to slither through the air and land beside Dragon in his human form. The *shi shi*, with Rosamund on its back, leapt over as well.

There were Wugong, a faintly visible woman Tiger guessed must be Wugong's partner, the living *shi shi* statue, and the eight others; Stephanie, Simon, Gilly, William, Robby, Rosamund, Chou and Hoshi. Four of them marked—according to Dragon—by the younger Gods of Khaitan's eight Immortals. Did that mean the other four were marked as well? Or were they involved for other reasons?

"Tiger. Do not daydream. We must decide what to do and I need your full attention."

With an abashed grin and a rueful glance at Robby, Tiger agreed. "What's the plan?"

"First, we require space to think. Gilly, can you keep those others away from us? Especially the hag. I do not want her to get her claws on Robby's little friend."

"I don't either." Robby opened his mouth to continue the thought, no doubt at length, but Dragon's expression warned him and—for once—he took the hint.

At the same time, Gilly curled round them, forming a protective circle of smoke and fire that was only mildly uncomfortable for those within. "Do you want me to eat anyone?"

Both William and Dragon answered, "NO." Tiger thought Gilly was joking but was glad the former monster had been told to behave. Gilly was dangerous and troublesome, but he generally accepted limitations; mostly because it suited him to do so.

Beyond the wall of smoke and fire coiled protectively around them, Tiger could hear the sound of angry shouts as their enemies tried to break through. Horne's voice was getting rougher, and Tiger suspected the man was slowly losing his humanity as the rift energies twisted through him.

Dragon caught Tiger by the earlobe to get his attention. "Now. I have been shown what all of you have experienced today. I know some of you have been granted aid from four of Khaitan's Immortals. The rest of you have various parts to play in all this as well, though exactly what I can't say."

"If Horne and Andersen pay for what they've done, we could set all this to rest," Wugong's partner pointed out.

"While I would love to simply act on that," Dragon answered, "It won't break the tie between this place and Khaitan. Besides, whatever they have done, American law demands trial and judgment. We have time for neither."

"Exactly the sort of thing I'd expect from you, you useless—" Wugong stopped when he found both Robby and Chou right in his face. "What the—"

"Another word," Robby said in Cantonese, "Just one more word. And I promise you'll have fewer teeth to say it with."

"Not to mention a broken nose," Chou added grimly.

"Both of you stand down," Dragon ordered. "Any teeth and nose breaking will be between Wugong and myself." With everyone silenced, she continued, "Yahgmar, I am given to understand the thing stolen from your village was a *daitsushi* ?"

Unwillingly, the Batsu ghost agreed. "Half was held within the sphere our male *shi shi* guarded. The other half is in the cub." She indicated Robby's small companion.

Chou went white as a sheet. "There's a *daitsushi* in the cub? I transformed a *daitsushi*? *ahyiaaahhhh!*"

"Shhh, boy. You survived." Dragon waved off Chou's panic without bothering to look at him. "Tiger, is it possible the rift our friend Horne controlled was created by a *daitsushi*?"

"More than possible." Tiger examined the blackness roiling around inside Hoshi's device and spotted something glimmering at its center. He pointed at it. "Right there. I think that's why he's after me."

Dragon peered into the device as well. "Indeed. Then I see only one solution. I must take the cub to Khaitan. I, Chou, Robby, Hoshi and Rosamund."

"Wait. What? No. You can't—" That was Gilly, twisting around so his huge black head was looking into the circle his body created. "I forbid it."

"Will you have her home turned to another Khaitan, this time without Gods to defend it from the void?" Dragon's question made the former monster wilt a little. "You are barely on the High Road, old one. You know you are not up to the task."

"But why Rosie?"

"Not that I mind," Rosamund added. "But yes. Why me?"

"Your talent for speaking to beasts, child. The cub can show the path through the void to Batsu Village in Khaitan, but you are the only one who can understand her. Besides, once you are there, you will be the guide by which Gilly seeks you out."

"I? Seek her out?" Gilly hesitated, then understanding dawned. "Oh. You want me to bring us all to Khaitan after them."

Dragon inclined her head, "Once we are gone, you must take up positions at the corners of this roof. William to the northeast, Gilly to the northwest—"

"Which puts me and Miss Frazier in the southeast and the southwest respectively," Simon stated. "Given we're supposed to be in the same position as our sponsoring God?" Beside him, Stephanie swallowed, then tightened her grip on her weapon and looked determined.

Approvingly, Dragon inclined her head, then pointed. "The *shi shi* must take his place here, just as his daughter will take her place on the other side of the rift."

Stephanie agreed, though her eyes were wide with fear. "I'll do my best."

"You would not have been chosen if you could do anything less," Dragon reassured her. She turned to Robby. "You carry Miss Rosamund. I will ride with Chou and Hoshi. Meng can handle the three of us."

Firmly, Hoshi disagreed, patting her little helicopter. "I'll take my Iron Dragonfly, Dragon. It can handle the rift the same way Robby's motorcycle can."

Before anyone could object, Hoshi mounted her toy and with a sigh, Dragon gestured at the others. "Well? Are you waiting for an invitation?"

The cold of the rift set a chill in Dragon's bones. She ignored it, clinging to Chou and keeping her eyes half closed against the howling wind surrounding them. She'd learned years ago not to look too closely at what lay outside the worlds. Call it Chaos, call it the void, call it the rift; it was not the place for human minds to contemplate too closely.

Then, to her relief, intense purple blackness gave way to bright sunlight and desert sands. That was right, it might be near midnight in Strikersport, but it was still day here in Khaitan. She was about to order the youngsters to find Batsu village when a plane—painted the eight bright colors of Khaitan's flag—zoomed past them, its pilot gesturing for them to follow.

"Feng Zhanchi." Dragon smiled, guessing her old friend must have been told to expect them. Even if the Gods didn't warn their land's Air Force Commander, one of Khaitan's mages would have sensed the approach of strangers through the void. They must not have looked a threat, fortunately, or Zhanchi would have brought along a squad or so of dragons and firebirds.

As they all landed in the sands of Khaitan's Northwestern desert, Zhanchi leapt out of his plane and rushed at his daughter, picking her up and swinging her around gleefully. "Did you build that? It's beautiful. Let me fly it, right?"

"I did, yes it is, and later." Normally Hoshi looked more like the sedate American-Japanese woman climbing out of Zhanchi's plane, but right then her father's blood was clear in her broad grin. "It's good to see you, papa."

Hikaru, Itinerant Magistrate of the Western Province and Dragon's best friend, approached them. Her expression was calm as she inclined her head to her daughter, but they didn't embrace. She wore the robes and hat of a Judge and that meant she was there on official business. Which, in turn, meant Hikaru knew what was happening.

Rather than waste time with pleasantries and ignoring Zhanchi as he reacquainted himself with Robby and Chou and met Rosamund, Dragon went to Hikaru. "We have little time, old friend. Where is Batsu village?"

"Just over that dune, Dragon. If I understand matters correctly, the dead of that village seek justice on their killers in Strikersport?"

That being exactly correct, Dragon simply agreed. "I believe the only way we're going to resolve this is if we bring the—"

A roar of maternal outrage drew everyone's attention as a stone lion rushed over the ridge. The female of the pair, her protective instincts aroused by the scent of her cub. Panicked, Dragon raced to intercept her, intending what, she didn't know. "Robby! Look out!"

"Oh, do please wait," Rosamund said suddenly. "See, your baby's just fine. Here. You can have him. Robby, give her her baby."

Robby opened his mouth to argue but Dragon gently removed the cub from his jacket and offered her to her mother, who'd skidded to a halt at Rosamund's plea. "There is no need to be angry. The cub is unharmed."

The cub mewled rapidly, telling her side of the story and somehow Dragon knew when she told her mother about Chou's transformation spell. The mother turned a furious gaze on the boy and once again Dragon moved to put herself in the lion's way. "It was to protect the cub," she said firmly. "No harm was done."

Again the cub mewed and, unwillingly, the lioness relaxed, making a questioning noise Rosamund translated as, "Where is my husband?"

"He is back where we came from. But if you and your cub, and Miss Rosamund here, will help, he should be returned to your side soon." Dragon turned her attention on Hikaru again, "The Feast of Hungry

Ghosts begins in Strikersport. This business has created a link between this place and our home. We can use that to pull everyone involved here. You are in charge of this province. Will you permit?"

"I permit," Hikaru said gravely.

Bowing, Dragon turned to the others. "Robby, you take the north side. Chou, the east. Hoshi, you're south and Rosamund, you take west." She guided them into position, calculating the distance they'd need between them.

"Well, all right, but I don't understand. Do you understand, Flopsy?" That was addressed to the cub, who cocked its head at her and mewled something. "Oh. Because I'm standing in for Meng Huang Hsiang? Wait. Who is Meng Huang Hsiang?"

Hikaru arched an eyebrow at the girl but didn't ask questions. Instead she dragged her husband out of the center of the circle. Nor did Dragon bother explaining that the Gods, being unable to manifest themselves in the physical world without hurting everyone around them, needed someone compatible to take their part. Rosamund, being half-mad in some respects, was an excellent anchor for the god of Delusions. Just as Robby could anchor the Northern King, Chou the Eastern Dragon and Hoshi the Southern Queen. Each shared some small resemblance to the God they stood in for.

"Little lion cub," Dragon called. "Mama *shi shi*. I need your help." She drew the curved central line of the circle and beckoned the pair to the northwestern side. "Your toy is on the other side, baby. Call it, and your father, here. Rosamund, give Gilly your thoughts. The rest of you, stay focused."

Then Dragon drew on Khaitan's magic and opened the way.

It wasn't long after Dragon and the others left that Gilly began to falter. The former monster was strong, but he'd been working hard for much of the day and he was tiring. Tiger, recognizing Gilly was at the end of his rope, ordered, "Change back. You can't hold them much longer."

"The—hell—I—can't—" Gilly tried to argue.

"The hell you can," William retorted. "Do as you're told."

"You're not—the boss—of—me—"

"I outrank you, Officer Kenneth. Turn human and stop trying to do it all alone."

With a sigh, Gilly obeyed, dropping to the rooftop in one corner. Fortunately, he wasn't the enemy's target. They were all more interested in getting at Tiger and the thing he held. Well, that and ripping each other to shreds.

"Is it just me," Stephanie said suddenly, "Or are they all monsters? Except for Mr. Andersen and that woman?"

Tiger looked closely at the people fighting around them, using his sting every so often for protection. "It's not just you." The Centipedes were still human, but they'd wisely decided to cower around the edge of the rooftop, clearly not wanting anything to do with the others. The other gangs: from Boston and Bear Gulch, had transformed.

The Boston gang was now some sort of strange mix of insect and human. "Gdzari," Yahgmar whispered behind him. "Sand slayers. They hunt the desert near our village. Or used to. Oh, Taranga, how could you do this thing?"

Tiger didn't have an answer to that. Nor did he need one, because that was when a ball of pure black chaos formed across from him. Remembering what Dragon had said, he shouted, "Everyone to your places! Quickly!"

As the others obeyed, the roof shuddered under Tiger's feet. The device in his hands heated up, Hoshi's pattern shining bright as the energy it held reacted to the other sphere. Automatically, Tiger adjusted the controls and tightened his grip.

Sunlight streamed over them suddenly as the rooftop shifted from one reality to another and Tiger had to force himself to stand upright until things settled. He never minded traveling the rift itself, but this sort of instantaneous twist in the Way Things Were always made him dizzy.

The light of Khaitan had a clarity to it that made it obvious they weren't in the human world anymore. As always he felt like Dorothy staring in wonder at the technicolor paradise of Oz. Then he was forced to focus on the thing in his hands. He had a feeling it was their only way back. Except Hoshi's device was losing power, the energy it needed to maintain control of the thing was immense and it hadn't been built to handle a rift, much less handle one for this long.

Suddenly the male *shi shi* was there, catching the sphere in its mouth and holding it tight. "Are you sure?" Tiger asked and it glared at him.

"That's what it was created for," Gilly answered, looking around for Rosamund. "More power to it."

Relieved, Tiger shut the device off, leaving the *daitsushi* to the *shi shi's* more than capable jaws and looking around to see what needed done.

The answer being not much. Simon and Stephanie had teamed up, the one distracting attackers with his borrowed shadows while the other hit them with Sun Wukong's staff. Rosamund rejoined Gilly and happily encouraged him as he tripped ogres and rift-infected thugs headfirst into the sand. Robby and Chou were arguing genially over who'd done what to whom while Hoshi and Zhanchi supplied air support. Even Wugong helped out, if only to keep himself alive.

In fact, the only ones not actively involved in the fight were William, Headwoman Yahgmar, Dragon and Hikaru. Seeing things were as controlled as they could be, Tiger went to join his partner. "This is a bit of a mess. What do we do to stop it?"

"The main problems appear to be the hag and the man—if he can be called that anymore—named Horne." Hikaru pointed from one to the other. "The hag, and the *gdzari* are all under Taranga's control. If she can be persuaded to dismiss them, our troubles may be halved."

Dragon considered the fight. "Tiger, keep Horne occupied. I'll deal with Taranga, as her mother is no longer corporeal enough to do so."

Having watched Dragon raise their children, Tiger had no doubt she was up to the challenge.

Dragon searched out the woman who'd called herself Minerva. Now she looked closer it was easier to see how much of Taranga's appearance was artifice. Light make-up to conceal desert-bronzed features, bleach to lighten brownish-gold hair to a brassy shade. Lipstick to round out thin lips, and a careful selection of high class finery to make those who saw her think she was just another westerner. Unlike Yahgmar and the spirit who'd possessed Rogers, she was no ghost but a living, breathing woman.

"I'm telling you, I expect an explanation for this nonsense." Mr. Andersen displayed a fine talent for ignoring circumstances. Even Wugong would understand he'd fallen into a mess of supernatural danger. Dragon wondered if Andersen was one of Taranga's monsters like his wife. No wonder the woman couldn't retain a simple fact like the difference between a *fu* dog and a *shi shi*. Taranga had been lucky her monster had managed to put her clothes on straight, much less control the urge to eat everyone in sight.

After a moment of consideration, Dragon concluded that Andersen was a normal human. He was just that oblivious to the situation. Unable to comprehend a world where he wasn't the most important person, he couldn't connect the events around him to an actual threat. If Taranga wasn't using the *gdzari* to block Horne's men, Andersen would have been dead several times over.

The trouble with using nearly brainless monsters as tools was they could be terribly rigid in their actions. Just as the hag couldn't remember the right word for *shi shi*, the *gdzari* were only guarding Taranga from active dangers. Which made it easy for Dragon to step past them, hands loose and unthreatening, until she was right beside Andersen and Taranga.

"What happened to my wife? Do you have something do with this? Why are they attacking us?"

Dragon answered for the woman. "Your wife was a monster—"

"Tell me something I didn't know."

"I mean a true monster, a creature bound by magic and created by belief." Dragon pointed at the hag as she ripped Horne's arm from his shoulder. Not that it did any good. Horne just grew a new one, grinning smugly as he did so. Rather than continue the argument, Dragon turned her attention on Taranga. "Have your monsters stand down. Dismiss them. Do something to rid us of them. It's time we dealt with this situation, before something worse happens than an uncontrolled rift."

"I will not! I'll have my vengeance! I will kill them all. Thieves! Murderers! They'll pay—"

Without bothering to argue another moment, Dragon punched the woman in the nose, dropping her on her butt before she could say another word. "You've stolen what was not yours and murdered innocent bystanders. You have nothing to stand on and no right to complain."

Something moved behind Dragon, a towering mass of purple-black ooze that twisted and squirmed as it rose over her. She spun out of its way, as Tiger came in from behind, thrusting his cane into its surface and sending a jolt of energy through the entire amorphous mass. Dozens of voices screamed as the stuff collapsed and melted away, leaving its contents—Horne's Bear Gulch gang—sprawled in the desert sand. Only one was strong enough to rise to his feet, gun in hand.

Before the man could fire, Tiger gave him a good solid punch to the jaw, dropping him to the ground. "I'd suggest staying down," Tiger said calmly. "Before you get yourself in worse trouble."

"Release them." Yahgmar scolded, appearing before Taranga in a flash. "Release them now, daughter. You've caused more than enough trouble."

The sorceress stared at the ghost with wide eyes. "Mother? You? You're still here?"

"I was right beside the Centipede master, girl. I did not change my face as you have. You ought to have known me then." The ogre clawed at the ghost, fingers sweeping through her unhindered. "Stop your servants, Taranga. Now. You've done enough!"

Taranga gasped, "Stop. Enough. No more." It didn't work. The hag and the *gdzari* kept fighting, which meant Horne and his men wouldn't stop either. "No. Don't do that! I'm ordering you to stop!"

Realizing Taranga had lost control of her slaves, Dragon called out, "Get back! Stay away from those things. Tiger, you know what to do."

They'd practiced the maneuver so many times, though never against opponents so big or so fast. She, racing up the hag's backside and kicking her behind the ear. He going low, to break Horne's kneecap with his cane.

To Dragon's surprise, she found Tiger climbing up the hag's other arm, claws crackling with electricity as he grabbed the monster by the nape of the neck. Tiger, but not her partner, she realized. The young one, the one not allowed to work in Strikersport itself anymore. The boy was going to get himself killed someday, but right then Dragon was grateful. She was getting too old for this kind of nonsense.

As the hag shrieked and fell to the ground, twitching, Dragon saw the other, younger, Dragon helping her Tiger, breaking Horne's jaw with a well aimed blow from a weighted sleeve. As the second monster went down, they landed close by, turning to protect each others' backs.

Except the attack had done its work. Horne was once more in human form, groaning as he tried to sit up and failed. As for Mrs. Andersen, she melted away to nothing as they watched. Even better, without their leaders, the *gdzari* and Horne's men no longer had reason to fight. They sat down and stared blankly, unsure what to do.

Someone applauded as he approached them. Feng Zhanchi, grinning broadly as he walked behind his wife.

"Well done, Dragon."

"Thank you, Magistrate Feng."

Hikaru surveyed the mess. "You seem to have brought me an interesting problem."

"Indeed."

"Criminals all over the place. Some of whom belong quite firmly elsewhere." Hikaru eyed the men thoughtfully. "I wish the full story now. Everything you know, please, not just the highlights."

The story took some time in telling, by which time Khaitan's sun had set, so Hoshi lit the scene with one of her stars. It glittered above them, a complex and beautifully intricate design that had the *shi shi* cub fascinated. Even its parents sat and stared with unblinking, interested eyes.

At last Hikaru looked over the crowd. "Those of you touched by our Gods, I thank. Your actions have helped prevent a shattering of the walls that would damage both our worlds."

"No problem, ma'am," Gilly said cheerfully. "It was just about the most fun I've had in a while." He stopped at Dragon's dour look, though his grin said he was only silent because he was too tired to push his luck.

"Most of these men belong to your world and your world's law," Hikaru continued as if Gilly hadn't spoken. "Those two, however, are a problem." She pointed at Horne and Andersen. "These men were the ones who attacked and slaughtered the people of Batsu—"

"I'm an American citizen, girlie!" Horne growled. "You have no power over me."

"Over either of us," Andersen added haughtily.

"You are American citizens, yes," Hikaru agreed equably. "I could not extradite you while you remained on American soil. However, this is not America and American law does not apply. Khaitan has no treaty with your lands to protect you from the consequences."

Andersen looked around wildly and his eyes lit on William. "You! You're the police. You can't let them—"

"I don't know," William spread his hands. "I'm just a minor cop in a tiny podunk city. I don't have any international authority. There might be a diplomat willing to discuss the matter with Khaitan's government, but I'm afraid my hands are tied."

"Yes. That's it. My vengeance—"

Hikaru turned on Taranga. "Do not be so smugly sure of yourself. You are a citizen of Khaitan and your village has enjoyed our protection. Had you brought the matter to our attention we might have been able to take action. Instead you used and abused the powers of your God to call forth those who ought to have rested. You imposed your father's spirit on an innocent man to seek your vengeance. You brought danger to both Khaitan and the human world by tearing the fabric of reality. You, too, are guilty."

"I didn't cause the tear," Taranga protested.

"She's right on that count," Tiger added. "That's on Horne. He stole that *daitsushi* and used its power to build his weapon. I have a feeling he may have shared the technology with someone we ran across before."

Dragon frowned. "The Kranes and Timothy?"

"That makes sense," the younger Tiger said. "I wondered." He went silent and she looked at him, marveling at his ability to hold his tongue. Maybe he should keep the mask on more often?

Considering the elder Tiger's statement, Hikaru agreed. "Then I will not blame you for that, Taranga."

"Her hag killed one of our family," the younger Dragon said. "Don't let her off entirely."

"I will not, child. I promise." Hikaru turned to Yahgmar. "You joined with a criminal—"

Yahgmar bowed her ethereal head. "I did. I needed an assassin and he was willing to help me."

"Didn't kill anyone this time. Well, maybe a few of those thugs," Wugong protested. "Be fair, sister-in-law—"

"I am Itinerant Magistrate Feng of the Western Province, Feng Wugong. Our relationship doesn't matter." Hikaru sighed. "But it is true that I must recuse myself in your case. You will answer for what you've done, just not to me."

Wugong muttered, "And how are you planning on keeping me— oh—" The last was said as he realized they were now surrounded by Khaitanese soldiers, all armed with swords and crossbows. "Fine. Fine. Whatever."

Returning her attention to Dragon, Hikaru said, "It would be well, I think, for you to to return to Strikersport soon."

Dragon bowed. "Time and more than time to do so." She called the *shi shi* to her, requesting their aid. "Until later, Hikaru."

"Until later, Dragon. Be safe and be well. And keep an eye on my daughter."

The night sky shifted as the *shi shi* used their power to return the wanderers to the rooftop of Trendle Tower. She turned her attention on the others, making sure they were all unhurt and was unsurprised to see younger Tiger holding the *shi shi* cub.

"She came to me," the youngster told her pleadingly. "I didn't ask her to."

Dragon sighed. "I will discuss this with you later. For now, we must all clean up this mess. After all, there's a Festival to prepare for and very little time with which to do so."

Rosamund straightened. "And, oh no. My charity ball!"

With yet another sigh, Dragon told the young woman, "Will have to wait until things have been repaired and cleaned. Which," she glared at the younger Tiger and Dragon, "they will be, will they not?"

The youngsters eyed each other and—for once—agreed without argument.

Epilogue

"Do you lot really think you're fooling anyone?" Michaels asked Cheh Chang as he sat watching a long, and growing longer, dragon dance through the banquet hall. "I mean, it's obvious—"

"Obvious, perhaps, to those who know us," Chang admitted, chuckling to himself. "But our agreement does still stand. This last bit of foolishness only involved us by chance. And those foolish young 'Claws of the Golden Dragon' did keep their promise not to act within Strikersport proper."

Michaels sighed, looking frustrated. "I know, I know. You didn't bring any of that lot here and you did your best to make sure as few civilians would be hurt as possible. But yegads and little fishies, man. Are we going to have this happen all the time?"

"I warned you last year that magic tends to congregate. There's not so much here as to be a problem yet, but—" Chang spread his hands, helplessly. "It is out of my control. And are you not happier, knowing there are those able and willing to act against evil when it comes to us?"

"What happens to that lot that got gifted, though?"

"The one has walked further up the high road, or so I am told. Gilly could still fall, but he has two worshippers to give him reason not to. As for the other three; they have learned valuable skills. What they do with that knowledge is something I cannot answer. Yet."

Fretting, because it was in his nature to do so, Michaels said, "I just don't want more trouble."

"Trouble is a thing none of us can avoid. This is a chancy world we live in, Chief Michaels. Chancy and dangerous." Chang smiled as he watched his grandsons run across the stage, Chou dressed as Sun Wukong, while Robby chased him, garbed in the Heavenly Warrior Erlang Shen's armor. "Best, I think, to have strong arms and brave hearts to stand against that evil. No matter how aggravating they may be otherwise."

THE END

ABOUT OUR CREATORS

AUTHOR -

BARBARA DORAN—has been making up stories for as long as she can remember. From playing Ms. Marvel to her best friend's Captain Marvel to writing new stories for old characters (Hannibal King, X-Men, Green Hornet, The Saint, The Shadow and many others), to writing gaming and anime fanfiction online.

After ten years behind the keyboard as a software engineer, Barbara realized that her true love wasn't coding but making stuff up. So when she left that career in favor of dealing with two frequent interruptions of her life (namely her own personal Tiger and Dragon), she decided to use what little time they allowed her to work on writing. Her Long Suffering Husband, without whom she could never have managed such a goal, has been nothing if not supportive.

Along with reading every mystery, SF and fantasy book she could get her hands on, Barbara grew up watching Star Trek, Batman, Green Hornet, along with the usual Saturday morning cartoons. She became addicted to shows like Battle of the Planets and Doctor Who in her teens and discovered Run Run Shaw's martial arts flicks some years later. Those influences, along with a love of folklore and mythology, have become part of the world some small portion of her mind lives in. When, of course, she isn't chasing Tiger and Dragon from one school event to another.

Barbara can be contacted at <BarbaraDoran@sumergoscriptum.com>. Her website is <http://www.sumergoscriptum.com/barbaradoran/>.

COVER ARTIST -

ROB DAVIS—began his professional art career doing illustrations for role-playing games in the late 1980s. Not long after he began lettering and inking, then penciling comics for a number of small black and white comics publishers- most notably for Eternity Comics, which eventually became Malibu Comics in the 1990s, on their book SCIMIDAR with writer R.A. Jones. Branching out to other black and white publishers and eventually working at both DC and Marvel Rob worked on likeness intensive comics like TV adaptations of QUANTUM LEAP and STAR TREK's many incarnations mostly on the DEEP SPACE NINE comics for Malibu. At Marvel he worked on the Saturday morning cartoon adaptation PIRATES OF DARK WATER.

After the comics industry implosion in the late 1990's Rob picked up work on video games, advertising illustration and T-shirt design as well as some small press comics like ROBYN OF SHERWOOD for Caliber. Rob continues to do the occasional self-published comic book as well as publisher and designer for his small-press production REDBUD STUDIO COMICS. Rob is Art Director, Designer and Illustrator for the New Pulp production outfit AIRSHIP 27 partnered with writer/editor Ron Fortier. Rob is the recipient of the PULP FACTORY AWARD for "Best Interior Illustrations" in 2010 and 2015 for his work on SHERLOCK HOLMES: CONSULTING DETECTIVE and has been nominated for the same award every year since the award's inception. He works and lives in central Missouri with his wife and two children.

INTERIOR ILLUSTRATIONS -

GARY KATO—was born in Honolulu, Hawaii in 1949. He graduated from the University of Hawaii with a Bachelor of Fine Arts degree. His comic book work has appeared in such varied titles as DESTROYER DUCK, THUNDERBUNNY, MS. TREE and MR. JIGSAW. He's also illustrated children's books such as THE MENEHUNE OF NAUPAKA VILLAGE, and the currently available BARRY BASKERVILLE SOLVES A CASE, BARRY BASKERVILLE RETURNS and JAMIE AND THE FISH-EYED GOGGLES. He's also been a contributor to the Children's Television Workshop magazines, 3-2-1 CONTACT and KID CITY.